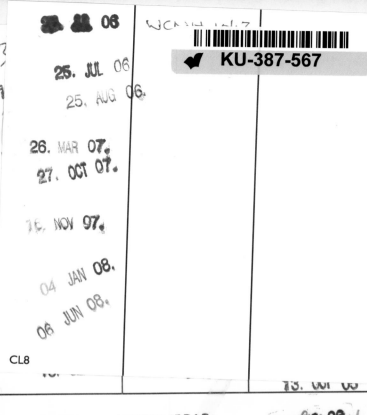

The Bandit Trail

The Bandit Trail

TOM PARRY

A Black Horse Western

ROBERT HALE · LONDON

© Tom Parry 1999
First published in Great Britain 1999

ISBN 0 7090 6556 6

Robert Hale Limited
Clerkenwell House
Clerkenwell Green
London EC1R 0HT

Typeset in North Wales by
Derek Doyle & Associates, Liverpool.
Printed and bound in Great Britain by
WBC Book Manufacturers Limited, Bridgend.

For Anne, Allan, Glyn and Kerry

Chapter 1

Rosita's dance increased in tempo as the fiddlers quickened their playing. The other dancers had all moved back to form a circle and now began to clap in time to the music. Her high heels beat a rhythmic tattoo on the rough stage which had been erected to hold the five musicians. She was on the front of the stage with her skirt twirling as she spun, stamped and paused in a typical Mexican dance. The comb in her jet-black hair caught the sunlight as she moved. There was a slight smile on her full red lips and she held her head proudly. She was wearing a tight-fitting black shirt which showed the roundness of her breasts to their best advantage. Her full, multi-coloured skirt was one moment wrapped round her legs, and the next flying open to reveal her sun-tanned legs.

No one at the barbecue could take their eyes off her. The men, Mexicans and Americans alike, eyed her lasciviously, while the women regarded her enviously. Even the Mexican soldiers who were standing around seemed to forget that they were on duty and that they were being paid to guard their host, Señor Garcia, and his wife and their two sons. They were leaning on their carbines and some were licking their lips with desire as they watched Rosita.

Luke Ballard was watching her with mixed feelings. On the one hand he was admiring the expertise with which she was bewitching the onlookers with her dancing. On the other hand he couldn't help feeling a pang of jealousy. Rosita had pledged last night that she was his true love, yet here she was, flaunting herself in front of those attending the barbecue. He studied her lips, which almost had a curl of disdain on them, and he remembered how he had kissed them for what had seemed hours last night.

One other thing was worrying Luke. This was not his heart, but another part of his anatomy, his stomach. This morning he had eaten for breakfast a plateful of tortillas together with generous helpings of chilli sauce. His taste buds had told him that they were delicious, but now his stomach was telling him that he shouldn't have eaten them. He knew that he would soon have to pay a visit to the latrines at the far end of the field.

He delayed going in order to try to see the end of Rosita's dance. But she was still holding her audience enthralled. She was putting great controlled effort into the dance yet Luke couldn't see any perspiration on her brow. He glanced across at Señor Garcia and his family. It was rumoured that he was the richest man in the town of San Caldiz. He certainly had a splendid villa with extensive grounds and he definitely knew how to look after his guests and staff – as the piled-up plate which Luke had emptied for breakfast could have testified. Luke's gaze took in the soldiers. He noticed that they were no longer leaning on their carbines, but now held them at the ready. Perhaps their commanding officer, Captain Luis Salvari, had flashed them a warning with his eyes that they were neglecting their duty.

Luke knew that he could delay the inevitable no longer; he began to hurry towards the latrine. It was about a hundred yards away from the barbecue. When he reached the latrine he was aware that the music was still playing. Rosita's dance must still be in progress.

Afterwards, he quoted his favourite author, Shakespeare. 'For this relief much thanks'. He stepped out of the latrine and was instantly aware that the music had stopped. The sound that followed would be etched in his mind for the rest of his life. It was the sound of the soldiers shooting the Garcia family.

Chapter 2

Luke was sitting in Marshal Downley's office. Also in the office was Captain Manuel Torsa who represented the Mexican Section of the town. The captain was a short Mexican with a large curling moustache. The marshal, on the other hand, was a tall, taciturn Yankee in his fifties who had fought for the South in the Civil War twenty years before.

'I don't see how I can help you,' Luke stated, flatly.

'You have been working for Señor Garcia,' said Torsa, managing to convey that there was something sinister about somebody who worked for the late landowner.

'As a tutor – for his children,' added Luke.

'Exactly,' said Downley, leaning forward in his

armchair. 'You have spent weeks – no – months in the house, teaching the children. You must have seen something.'

'The two boys who are now dead,' said Luke, 'I have been teaching for the past six months, I have grown ... attached to them. Don't you think I want to see their killer brought to justice? Don't you think that, if there was some small clue as to the identities of the killers, I would give you the information gladly? But I don't know who was responsible. It all happened so suddenly. I can still hardly believe it happened,' he concluded, bitterly.

'You were Rosita's boyfriend, I believe,' said Torsa, silkily.

'How do you know that?' demanded Luke.

'I know most things that go on in San Caldiz,' purred Torsa.

'Then how is it you don't know who killed Señor Garcia, his wife and two children?' demanded Luke, hotly. He didn't like the oily Mexican, and he could conceal his dislike no longer.

Torsa flushed. 'There are some things that I do not know. But I intend to find out.' His small piggy black eyes bored into Luke.

Luke realized that he had probably made an

enemy for life of the Mexican chief of police, but so what? There was no future for him in this town now. He would clear up one or two loose ends and then head north into real American territory, not a border town like this where the Mexicans outnumbered the Americans by two to one.

'Have you been in touch with Rosita since the shooting?' demanded Downley.

'No,' admitted Luke, shortly.

'I find that rather strange,' said Torsa, speaking slowly to emphasize the point. 'You and Rosita were good friends. From what I hear you were very good friends. The shootings were three days ago. Yet you haven't got in touch with her.'

Luke was uncomfortably aware of the penetrating gazes of the two men. He didn't see what business it was of theirs. Anyhow, he had tried to contact Rosita, but she hadn't been at her lodgings. He had even tried to find one or two of the fiddlers who had been playing at the fiesta. They had been friends of hers. But they too had disappeared. Maybe they feared for their safety. Maybe Rosita also feared for her safety. It was true though, what the greasy Mexican sitting opposite had said. Luke had thought that he and Rosita were more than just good friends. The hours they had spent kissing under the trees the night before the killings had convinced him that their relationship was something special which could blossom into something fulfilling and lasting. But now his dream had been shattered by the killings and with Rosita's disappearance.

'Luis Salvari has disappeared together with the soldiers who were responsible for the killing,' stated Downley.

Luke already knew that. What was the marshal driving at? His next statement floored him.

'I believe that Salvari had also been a friend of Rosita's.'

At last he could see what they were driving at. Luke licked his lips which had suddenly gone dry. Yes, it was true that Salvari had been Rosita's boyfriend when he, Luke, had arrived to take up his position of tutor to the children. He had viewed their friendship with unconcern for the first few months, partly because he had been so busy with his tutorial duties. Then gradually he had become more and more aware of Rosita. He had thought that his interest in her had been returned by the way she smiled at him more often and by the few words of Spanish which they exchanged as they passed each other in the big house, or happened to be in the same room. Their friendship had blossomed; Salvari had disappeared into the background. A few nights ago, under the trees, he had been prepared to believe their friendship might change to love. Then had come the killings. And now the two men facing him were suggesting by their silence that Rosita was somehow mixed up in it.

'I don't believe she's got anything to do with the killings,' he retorted, angrily.

'You have to admit that it does seem rather convenient,' said Downley. 'Everybody is at the fiesta. They are watching Rosita dancing. All eyes are on her. Nobody is taking any notice of the soldiers, or Señor Garcia and his family. The soldiers open fire. All the family are killed at one stroke. It does look as though the whole thing was planned.'

'It doesn't mean to say that Rosita had anything to do with it,' protested Luke.

'When we find her we'll discover whether she did or not,' said Torsa. There was as much menace behind his words as in a basketful of rattlesnakes. In spite of the heat in the marshal's office Luke shivered. He had a pretty good idea how Torsa would make Rosita talk if she ever fell into his hands. He could only pray that when the law caught up with her, it would be the marshal who found her first. His gloomy thoughts were interrupted by the marshal's next words.

'Then there's Maria. She's disappeared too.'

'I was wondering what had happened to her,' said Luke. 'When I called round at the house yesterday, they said they didn't know where she was.'

'I had told my soldiers to say that,' said Torsa, smugly. 'They were carrying out my orders.'

'She wasn't killed as well, was she?' cried Luke, horrified at the thought of yet another tragedy befalling the Garcia family.

'She was lucky,' stated the marshal, bluntly. 'She was too ill to attend the barbecue. She was taken to the house of her aunt who lives just outside the town. And so escaped being killed.'

Luke heaved a sigh of relief. If he were a praying man he would have thanked the Virgin Mary for her deliverance.

'You were a member of the household,' said Torsa. 'It's strange that you didn't know that Maria was too ill to attend the fiesta. Does that mean to say that they didn't trust you with that knowledge?'

Luke would have given anything to have stood

up and smacked the smug Mexican in the face. Although he prided himself that he was not a violent man, he would have guaranteed he could have taken the smirk off his face. He had spent months as a trainee officer in preparation for a career in the cavalry; if he had learned nothing else, he had learned how to deliver a good straight right.

'Well?' Downley was waiting for an answer too.

'It was a big household. Sometimes we didn't see each other for days at a time,' said Luke, shortly.

'Don't you think that's strange?' asked Torsa.

'Not at all,' snapped Luke.

'I would have thought that if she was ill, you would at least have asked about her.'

'I did. I asked at breakfast time.' He was uncomfortably aware that both pairs of eyes were once again boring into his again as though trying to discover whether he was lying.

'I would have thought she would have liked to have seen the barbecue, even if she couldn't come down to it,' persisted Torsa. 'Her bedroom was above where they were holding it. She could have seen everything through her bedroom window. A young girl likes to watch exciting things going on down below.'

'She's not a young girl. She's seventeen,' said Luke, shortly.

'And were you teaching her too?' asked Downley.

'It was one of my duties. I was improving her English language, and teaching her literature.'

'Do you know why she was too ill to attend the barbecue?' asked Downley.

'I asked one of the maids,' admitted Luke. 'She said that she was suffering from a . . . woman's complaint.' Why was he almost blushing when he made the statement? It had more than a little to do with the fact that the two men sitting behind the desk were prying into matters which didn't concern them. He had already told them all he knew about the shootings. Which was exactly nothing. Why were they prying into the temporary illness of a sweet child like Maria? Why weren't they getting some soldiers together to hunt down Salvari and his Comancheros? He addressed the question to Downley. 'Why don't you go after Salvari? Why don't you get a posse of Texas Rangers together and hunt him down?'

For the first time since the questioning had begun Downley looked uncomfortable. 'To get a posse of Texas Rangers together I've got to have a good reason,' he exclaimed. 'There's a lot of politics coming into it. One of the reasons why the state governor would never sanction it is the fact that Señor Garcia was a Mexican.'

'And a notorious bandit,' supplied Torsa, smugly.

Luke was surprised. Shocked even. To think that he had been working for six months for a bandit. No, it couldn't be true, could it?

Downley was continuing with the explanation. 'You've only been here a short time. You do not know the background to the Garcia family. On the face of it Señor Garcia was the most prosperous landowner in the territory. But he got his wealth and land at a cost.'

'At the cost of hundreds of lives of honest Mexicans,' said Torsa, bitterly.

For the first and only time Luke felt a certain empathy with the chief of police.

'During the Civil War,' explained Downley, 'the army of which I was a part, wanted horses. Lots of them. As long as the horses were in good condition, nobody bothered to ask too many questions about how they came into the owner's possession. That owner was Garcia. He sold thousands of horses to us Yankees. Every one at a fat profit.'

'A far bigger profit than you would think,'

supplied Torsa. 'Since he stole them in the first place from farms south of the border.'

Luke was digesting this information and revising his opinion of Señor Garcia. True, he hadn't had much in the way of personal dealing with the man – his interview and subsequent appointment for his post had been carried out by the secretary, Luis Zapote. But somehow he had assumed that Señor Garcia was an established landowner whose pedigree went back for generations, possibly even as far back as the Spanish invasion. Indeed Señor Garcia had the aristocratic profile typical of the rulers of Spain at that time. And the painting of him which had hung in the hall had helped to further that impression. Now Luke had discovered that Garcia was nothing more than a horse-thief.

'All right, that will be all, Mr Ballard,' the marshal was saying, dismissively.

It took a few moments for the remark to sink in, so busy was Luke with his own thoughts. Finally he stood up.

'Will you be leaving San Caldiz?' asked Torsa.

Somehow the enquiry now seemed just a friendly one. It wasn't a loaded question like some of the earlier ones he had received.

'There's nothing to keep me here now, is there?' Luke Ballard said, as he went out through the door.

Chapter 3

Luke made his way back to the villa with no definite idea what his next move would be. He would, of course, attend the funerals of Señor Garcia and his family tomorrow. After that, since there was nobody to employ him, and he had nobody to teach – the thought struck him forcibly – he would pack up his bags and leave San Caldiz.

He knew he would be running away. But from what? No, from whom, he corrected himself. Why, Rosita, of course. Maybe he should stick around and try to find her. In his imagination he could still feel the closeness of her body as she had clung to him a few nights before, and could still taste the passion of her kisses.

If he did stay he wouldn't know where to

start looking for her. She could have disappeared up into the hills, fearing for her safety, in which case he would never find her. Or, as the chief of police had suggested, maybe she had been involved in the killings. Perhaps she had been paid to become the focus of attention of those at the barbecue, so that the soldiers would have a comparatively easy task in killing Señor Garcia and his family.

No, he couldn't believe that. He couldn't believe she would be involved in the killings, even as a decoy. On the other hand, what did he know about her? Not a great deal. He didn't even know exactly what her duties in the household were. He had vaguely assumed that she was Maria's maid, since he had often seen her coming from Maria's room. But maybe he was mistaken about that. As it seemed he was mistaken about other things, he thought cynically, as he entered the villa and glanced at Señor Garcia's grand portrait which was hanging in the hall.

Luis Zapote was waiting for him in his room. Luke flushed with anger at the fact that the secretary had entered his room without permission. He had never liked Zapote. He had always reminded him of Uriah Heep in the Charles

Dickens book which he had read to Maria. Zapote was an excessively servile, smarmy bastard to his superiors, but at every opportunity he would treat the household staff under him like dirt.

However he had no opportunity to vent his anger on him, since Zapote's words took him by surprise. 'I have calculated that the family owes you twenty-five dollars in wages which you haven't been paid. I have made it up to thirty dollars, which I have placed on your desk. If you will kindly sign this receipt, we can consider the matter resolved.'

Luke's anger abated. He had been wondering whether he would receive the money which was owing to him. But now here it was. And it would come in useful until he found another position. He signed the receipt.

As Zapote was about to leave his room Luke asked, 'Do you know where I can find Maria?'

Zapote hesitated before replying. 'She's staying with her aunt just outside San Caldiz. She'll be here tomorrow for the funeral.'

Luke accepted the information with a slight inclination of his head. He didn't want to leave without saying goodbye to Maria. They had spent many happy hours together poring over the masterpieces of literature, not forgetting her favourite novel which was by a Spaniard, and entitled *The Adventures of Don Quixote*.

Luke spent the next few minutes packing. Not that he had many belongings, but what he did have he arranged neatly in an old battered saddle-bag which had been in his family for ages. His books, too, he stacked away carefully, with the exception of his volume of *Don Quixote*. He placed this on his dressing-table. He had decided to give it to Maria, suitably inscribed, in memory of their hours together.

What would he inscribe on the flyleaf? He was mulling over the wording while thinking about Maria. She had been the perfect pupil, always attentive and quick to see any unusual facet of the novel or poem which he would point out. She had a ready wit and would flash her wide smile at his remarks. Her lovely, large, luminous eyes would gaze at him while he read passages from his favourite poem or novel. She would grow up into a beautiful woman, intelligent, sensitive, compassionate. He realized this wasn't getting him any nearer writing the inscription on the flyleaf. Finally he wrote: *To Maria, a perfect pupil, in memory of the many happy hours we've spent together*. He signed it:

Luke Ballard.

Later in the day he was wandering casually around the town. It would be his last such stroll. In the six months he had been there he had come to like the dazzling white-plastered adobe buildings where the burning sun cast deep black shadows slicing them into startling shapes. He liked the cantinas with their low ceilings and shadowy interiors where time seemed to have stood still for generations. He came to the white church in the centre of the square with its tall bell-tower. After tomorrow he would no longer hear it tolling, calling the faithful to worship. He had never seen inside it, since he was not a Catholic, nor indeed a believer in any recognized religion. Maybe he should make one final effort to find out more about the god the Mexicans worshipped. But years following the path of religious dissent made him pass guiltily by.

Luke decided to have a final drink in his usual cantina. He had to duck his head to go through the doorway. He entered the long narrow room and Paco, the bartender looked up as he came in. There was one other person in the bar, a fat Mexican whose head was resting on a table as he slept. Luke ordered a whiskey

and told the barman to have one himself. After
all, he could afford to be generous; he had just
been paid off with thirty dollars.

The first inkling he had that things were not
as they seemed came when somebody entered
the bar and, as if in response to some kind of
signal, the fat man suddenly opened his eyes
and sat up. In itself this was not an unusual
happening, but Paco's reaction made Luke
instantly suspicious. Paco had disappeared into
the kitchen, though normally he would have
stayed and passed a few amicable sentences,
usually about the state of the weather. But the
alacrity with which Paco had made himself
scarce made Luke instantly alert to some kind
of danger. He guessed that it was in the form of
the newcomer into the bar.

Luke moved surreptitiously closer to the
bottle of whiskey that Paco had left on the bar.
In an emergency it could be a useful weapon, as
he had discovered on previous occasions in bar
brawls. When he was satisfied that he could
grab the bottle quickly if necessary, he turned
slowly and faced the newcomer.

He was a villainous-looking Mexican whose
appearance wasn't helped by a squint which
made him look even more sinister. It struck

Luke that if a play producer ever wanted someone to play a villain in one of Shakespeare's
plays then the man standing by the door would
be an ideal choice. Luke knew that at moments
of danger such a ludicrous thought would often
occur to him. Because there was no doubt that
he was in danger, as evidenced by the sudden
exit of Paco and the appearance of a knife in the
stranger's hand.

Luke licked his lips which had suddenly
become dry. Outside there was the sound of
dray-horses passing with their jingling chains.
It was funny how sound always seemed to
magnify when you were in danger of your life.
And Luke knew with sickening certainty that
the knife in the stranger's hand wasn't there for
peeling oranges.

The stranger advanced towards him. Luke
cast a quick glance in the direction of the fat
man. But sleeping beauty had moved to the
safety of a corner table, far away from any
sudden disturbance to the peace in the cantina.
Luke watched the advancing Mexican's eyes —
eyes always provided the clue as to when an
attacker would lunge. The Mexican advanced
with a crouching movement, his knife held at
the ready. It was a sharp-double-sided blade

29

which, Luke knew, if it ever came into contact with his flesh would slice through it as though it were butter.

Luke moved imperceptibly away from the bar. He waited until the Mexican was barely half a dozen feet away. He switched his glass of whiskey from his right hand to his left. This momentarily took the Mexican aback. Luke knew that it was now or never. He flung the contents of the whiskey glass into the Mexican's face. While the would-be assailant was blinking away the effects of the stinging spirit, Luke seized the whiskey bottle, stepped inside the faltering knife and brought the bottle down with all the force he could muster on the Mexican's head. The Mexican's eyes glazed, he uttered a choked groan and slid almost comically down to the floor.

Luke uttered the biggest sigh of relief he had uttered for months. He bent down and picked up the knife. A sudden movement behind him told him that although the first scene had finished, the act wasn't over yet. He spun round and was in time to see the fat man trying to sneak out through the door. Luke was just in time to seize him by the back of his shirt and drag him back into the bar.

'Where do you think you're going?' snarled Luke.

The fat man's eyes were big and round with fear. 'I don't know anything, *señor*, honestly,' he whimpered.

'I think you do,' snapped Luke. 'And I want some answers.' He held the knife close to the quivering fat man's Adam's apple. 'And if I don't get them, this knife is liable to slip and cause you to lose a lot of blood, understand?'

The fat man couldn't trust himself to speak. He could only nod.

'You recognized him the moment he came into the bar, didn't you?'

A nod.

'Then you'd better tell me who he is?'

'Velarde,' he croaked.

'And he doesn't operate on his own, does he?'

A shake of the head.

'So you're going to tell me the name of the gang he is a member of.'

The fat man glanced at the prone figure on the floor as if to convince himself that he really was still unconscious. 'He works for Señor Garcia's brother, Ricardo.'

'Ricardo the bandit?'

'*Si, Señor.*'

31

'Why should Ricardo send someone to attack me?' Luke addressed the question to himself.

The fat man gave an exaggerated shrug. 'Can I go now, *señor*? If he wakes up and finds me here, my life will not be worth a peseta.'

Luke removed the knife from the fat man's throat. He scuttled gratefully out through the door. As if on cue Paco reappeared behind the bar.

'What are we going to do with him?' demanded Luke.

'When he wakes up I will give him some free drinks,' said Paco. 'After that he will disappear and I will never see him again.'

'How do you know?' demanded Luke.

'It is simple, *señor*,' explained Paco. 'He knows that if he returns to the headquarters of the *bandidos* and tells Ricardo that he failed miserably in his attempt to kill you, then his own life will be forfeit. Ricardo doesn't suffer failures gladly.'

'Why would he want to try to kill me?'

'You are part of the Garcia family,' replied Paco. 'You have been living with them for six months. The soldiers probably had orders to shoot you with the family. When they didn't succeed they sent Velarde after you.'

'It seems that the sooner I leave San Caldiz, the better,' said Luke, as he watched Paco pouring their drinks.

Chapter 4

It seemed to Luke that half the population of San Caldiz was attending the funeral and had gathered in the cemetery. Many were also gathered outside the cemetery gates, waiting for the cortège to appear.

Luke had been expecting to see Maria in the villa, but she hadn't been down for breakfast. He had asked Zapote where she was, but had only received a frozen look in reply. It was obvious that he was no longer regarded as an accepted member of the household, and that after the funeral he would be expected to leave the vicinity *pronto*.

Among such a large crowd it was difficult to identify individuals, but he could see Marshal Downley standing just inside the gates, together with Captain Torsa, who was standing with a small knot of soldiers. Luke was wondering whether the fact that there were soldiers there on duty had any significance, as he listened to the mournful tolling of the church bell.

Luke was surprised how many graves bore marble statues. He knew that the Mexicans in the town were generally poorer than the Americans, yet it seemed that they were willing to spend considerable sums of money on the tombstones for their loved ones. He had been in similar cemeteries north of the border where the entire population of the town were Americans, and there was nothing in the graveyard to compare with the display of marble and ornamental stone he could see around him here.

The large crowd outside the gates fell silent and Luke guessed they could see the procession approaching. Sure enough in a few moments he himself could see, from his position inside the gates, the four black horses pulling the carriage. It was an apt touch, using black horses, thought Luke as he watched the carriage turn into the cemetery followed by the mourners. Yes, Maria was there, dressed in black and wearing a black veil. She was walking a few paces behind the carriage, accompanied by elderly women on either side whom Luke identified as her aunts, since he had seen them at the house on a few occasions. Luke couldn't see Maria's face because of the veil, but he guessed from her clenched fists and the way she walked with her head bowed, how much distress she was feeling.

The carriage stopped by the open grave. The *padre* stood there ready to start intoning his incantations. The family mourners spread out around the grave. Luke noticed with a feeling of revulsion that Zapote had taken up his position next to Maria. He had even taken hold of her arm – that degenerate slug daring to hold her arm. To Luke's relief she had shrugged him away, and moved to a position next to her aunts.

As Luke watched the coffins disappearing from sight into the earth he felt a huge sadness, not at the loss of Señor Garcia, or his wife, Carlotta, whom he had hardly met, but of the two boys, his pupils, whose lives had been so abruptly terminated. Why would anyone want to kill such innocent children? If whoever it had been had wanted to wreak their revenge on Garcia, why take it out on the children as well? Unless the *bandidos* who had wiped out the entire family had exceeded their instructions. Yes, that was possible. Maybe they weren't

supposed to have been killed, they had just
happened to be in the *bandidos'* line of fire.

Luke's gaze fell on Maria. He knew he was
regarding her for the last time. Their paths
would never cross again. He would go back to the
villa, collect his belongings and head north of the
border. Not that he had any definite idea where
it would be. But he was certain that it would be
far from San Caldiz. Maria, on the other hand,
would go back to her aunts' house, and probably
eventually marry some rich merchant or other,
since she would be an eminently marriageable
young lady, as they used to say in the Jane
Austen novels which Maria loved to read.

The *padre* was still intoning the funeral
service. Luke began to move slowly towards the
gates. There was nothing left for him to do here.
He had spent six months teaching the two children various points of English grammar, but
they had been killed, so in a sense it had been a
waste of time. True, though, he had instilled into
Maria a love of good poetry and literature. If he
had succeeded it was something which would
stay with her for the rest of her life. So maybe his
efforts hadn't been a waste of time after all.

He went out through the gates. He cast one
last glance at Maria. The funeral service was

over and they were starting to walk away from the grave. For a few seconds Luke could have sworn that Maria looked directly at him. They were a hundred yards apart, yet he could have sworn that she had held his gaze for a few moments. Her veil had been lifted from her face as she had wiped away a tear, and so he could see her face clearly. She had stared at him, hadn't she?

Luke's horse was tethered to a rail which the slow procession must pass to reach the Garcia villa. He watched its slow approach. He noticed that Zapote was still by Maria's side, although she had not taken his arm but was holding on to her aunts. Luke realized that he couldn't take his eyes off her. He was regarding her as intently as any love-struck youth would gaze at the person he loved. What nonsense was this? How could he be in love with her? She was only seventeen – only just out of pigtails. He couldn't have any feelings for her other than those of a teacher for his star pupil.

For the second time in a few minutes Luke was aware that Maria was staring directly at him. Now the procession had reached a position opposite to where he was waiting. Their eyes met and he was sure that she gave an almost imperceptible nod as she passed. Luke gave an acknowledging half-smile in reply.

It all happened so quickly. One minute the procession was wending its stately way along the road, and the next several horsemen appeared as if from nowhere. Before anyone knew what was happening one of them seized Maria. She kicked and struggled as he hauled her up into the saddle. The other horsemen were holding carbines in their hands to discourage any of the onlookers from attempting to rescue her. Nobody tried. In a few moments the horsemen were galloping away, with Maria being held tightly by the horseman who had seized her.

Chapter 5

Luke was in Marshal Downley's office. The marshal and Captain Torsa were seated while Luke was standing. He had been offered a seat, but had refused.

'Why didn't you have more soldiers on duty?' he flung the question at Torsa.

'We didn't expect anything to happen at the funeral,' replied Torsa.

Luke seized the implication. 'Ah, then you did expect something to happen,' he stated angrily.

'It was only a guess,' said Torsa, defensively.

'We thought that there might be trouble with Garcia's brother, Ricardo,' said Downley, mildly, in an effort to smooth some of the feathers of the irate teacher.

Luke didn't mention that Ricardo had sent one of his gang to try to kill him. It seemed unimportant compared with Maria's kidnapping.

'You knew that Ricardo had his brother and his family killed; you would expect him to try to finish off the remaining member of the family.' Luke hammered on the desk with his fist.

'We were going to keep a guard on the house,' asserted Downley. 'But we didn't expect Ricardo to make a move at the funeral.'

'No, I suppose not,' Luke admitted, wearily. 'The thing is, what are you going to do now?'

'What can we do?' demanded Torsa. 'Ricardo has disappeared into the hills. We would need a whole brigade of soldiers to attack his hiding-place. I have barely a dozen men. There is nothing we can do.'

'But you can't just leave her to her fate,' Luke stormed.

'If it is any consolation I do not think they will kill her,' stated Torsa.

'How do you know?' demanded Luke.

'If they had just wanted to kill her, they would have done so outside the cemetery. No, they have something else in mind for Maria.'

'You mean they kidnapped her as a hostage in order to demand money for her safe return?' Hope had sprung to Luke's heart with the suggestion.

'It's one possibility of course.' Torsa spread his hands wide.

What was the other possibility which hadn't been mentioned? Luke tried to keep his voice even as he asked the question.

'That he wants Maria as a wife,' stated Torsa.

'For himself?' Luke was aghast.

'No, for Ricardo's son, Paulo.'

Where had he heard about Paulo before? Luke racked his brains. Suddenly he had it. He and Maria had been reading the French novel, *The Hunchback of Notre Dame*. When they had come to the description of Quasimodo, Maria had burst out laughing. When he had asked her what was so funny, she had replied that it sounded like Paulo. She had informed him that her cousin was an ugly half-wit without anything to be said in his favour. And she could be forced to marry him! Luke's stomach turned over at the thought, 'Oh, no,' he groaned.

'It's just a possibility, of course,' said Torsa, disarmingly.

Luke felt that it was more than a possibility – it was a probability. He remembered something else that Maria had said when they had read more of the novel. She had said that Paulo had always wanted to play with her when his father,

Ricardo, had brought him to the villa. She had always avoided his presence by pretending to be sick. But one day he had come upon her unexpectedly in the garden. He had tried to kiss her. She had struggled and managed to run away. He was a clumsy oaf who didn't stand a chance of catching her. But he had shouted after her something which had chilled her blood. He had shouted, 'One day you'll be my wife!'

The statement was now chilling Luke's blood.

Luke was seeking refuge from the terrible pictures which kept flooding his mind of the lovely Maria struggling to escape from a Quasimodo-like figure. He was seeking refuge in Paco's cantina. There was nobody else in the bar.

'You are leaving San Caldiz?' Paco addressed the question to Luke. He had noticed through the open door when Luke had arrived on his horse that a saddle-bag was strapped to the back of the saddle.

'I suppose so. There's nothing for me here.' Luke downed his fifth whiskey. 'Ricardo has captured Maria,' he added, although he guessed that Paco already knew what had happened. News spread like wildfire in the town.

'They say he intends to make her marry

Paulo,' stated Paco. A few seconds after making the remark he wished he hadn't done so, since the tall American had lifted him effortlessly off his feet. He was held so that his face was almost touching the American's.

'Don't ever talk about Maria and Paulo in the same breath,' hissed Luke. 'Or I will personally see to it that your wife will not be having any more children by you. Savvy?'

Paco nodded. He could do no more since his shirt was held tightly round his neck preventing any other method of communication. Luke stared at him thoughtfully before putting him down. 'Have a drink,' he said, as though nothing untoward had happened, pushing the bottle towards the barman.

'Thanks,' said Paco.

After the episode Luke lapsed into a melancholy study, while Paco wisely refrained from talking.

'Where would he take her to?' Luke asked finally.

'There is a valley many miles from here. About three days' ride,' ventured Paco. 'His *bandidos* live there.'

'How would I get there?' demanded Luke.

Paco recognized the belligerent tone returning

to the teacher's voice. 'It would not be safe for you to go there, *señor*,' he replied, placatingly. 'Even if you could find a guide.'

Luke mulled over the possibility of reaching the bandits' hide-out. The chances were so slender that they weren't even worth considering. He downed another whiskey, but it made no difference. The odds were still about a thousand to one.

'I suppose Captain Torsa would know where the valley is,' Luke ventured, thoughtfully.

'*Si, señor*,' replied Paco. 'But he would never risk his men on such a venture. They could all be wiped out in one ambush.' He moved further from the bar in case the mad American's arm shot out and lifted him again.

But Luke was too busy selecting and rejecting possibilities. 'What I want,' he said, finally, slurring his words slightly, 'is a map.'

'A map would help,' agreed Paco, lugubriously.

'A map of this valley,' Luke brightened somewhat as he considered the idea. 'Has it got a name?'

'The Valley of the Poppies, *señor*.'

'Poppies?' Something clicked in Luke's mind. The difficulty was that he didn't make the connection which he knew was staring him in the face. 'Poppies,' he repeated, in an effort to come up with the answer.

'Even if you found the valley, you'd never come out of it alive,' warned Paco.

'Poppies, eh!' Luke thumped the counter, almost knocking the bottle of whiskey over. 'It's opium poppies, isn't it?'

'It would be worth more than my life is worth to tell you.' Fear had crept into Paco's expression.

'You don't have to. I know I'm right,' said Luke, excitedly. 'I was in the cavalry for eight months.' He didn't add that it had taken him eight days to find out that it was not the life for him. Afterwards, all he could do was to save up the hundred dollars which he had to find to get his release. While his companions were drinking, gambling and fornicating he would be staying in the barracks immersed in his books. It took him eight months to save up the money to buy his release. During that time he was the butt of the other soldiers' jokes, he was regularly picked upon to defend himself in fist fights. The result was that the experience made him physically harder. He could look after himself in a brawl. He could shoot straight, in fact he had won the annual award for shooting, much to the chagrin of his tormentors. The colonel of the regiment had pleaded with him to stay on in the cavalry, pointing out that he was definitely officer material. But Luke couldn't wipe the dust from Fort Manton quickly enough from his boots.

Among the activities the soldiers indulged in to relieve their boredom was taking opium. He had heard it said that about fifty per cent of the regiment was on the stuff. He had never tried it himself, nor was likely to do so. He knew about its addictive power from reading about the famous writers who became dependent on it, such as Coleridge, De Quincey and Edgar Allan Poe. He also knew that it was being supplied to the regiment by the Mexicans. The traditional poppy-fields of China had been partly forced out of business by the British. The high moral attitude of the Victorians in England had been rocked by the discovery that their most famous trading company, the East India Company, was making much of its money out of trading in opium, or its derivative, morphine. The British had blockaded the principal port, Canton, from which the opium was exported to Europe. This had left Mexico to take over much of the trade in the drug, since the climate was almost identical. They had seized their opportunity avidly. And now it seemed that Ricardo was the head man, the *jefe*, and he was growing the stuff in Poppy Valley.

'I know all about opium,' stated Luke. 'I saw what it could do to the men in the cavalry.'

'You were in the cavalry?' said Paco, wonderingly. It was obvious that he couldn't understand how someone who had been in the exalted position of being in the cavalry could have ended up by becoming a mere teacher.

Luke ignored him. He still had the problem of how to get to Poppy Valley. His mind had cleared with the excitement of the discovery that Ricardo was the head man who was supplying opium to the American soldiers. At that moment something happened which, if Luke had been a praying man, would have been the answer to his prayers. The trap-door behind the bar opened and a head appeared cautiously. It was the villainous-looking character who had tried to knife him yesterday. Luke assessed the situation more quickly than the Mexican. He dived behind the bar. Before the Mexican could close the trap-door, Luke had seized him by the collar and pulled him out.

'You are going to take me to Poppy Valley,' he stated in tones which brooked no argument.

Chapter 6

Velarde (that was the Mexican's name, Luke remembered,) accepted the situation quickly. Too quickly, Luke realized as they rode away from the town. Luke was on his white stallion and Velarde was incongruously by his side, riding a mule. Luke was reminded of Don Quixote and Sancho Panza, when they set out in Cervantes' *Don Quixote*, with Sancho Panza riding a donkey. But the villainous-looking character by his side bore no relation to the devoted Sancho Panza. Neither did he, himself, intend tilting at any windmills. Although he supposed that since the Don had set out to rescue Dulcinea, he could consider that he was in the same position with regard to Maria.

Luke had no illusions about the alacrity with

which Velarde had accepted the situation. The Mexican had reasoned that if he could kill Luke, as he had been instructed, then he could once again get back into Ricardo's favour. Who knew, perhaps Ricardo might even give him the desirable dancing girl Rosita, to show his appreciation. Velarde licked his thin lips in anticipation of the event.

The only thing he, Velarde, would have to be wary of was exactly where to kill the American. It was obvious that Ricardo would want evidence that the American was dead. This would mean bringing the American's corpse into the camp. It would be a tricky business riding his mule and leading the American's horse with the body tied to it. Therefore it would be better for him to wait as late as possible – say when they were within a couple of miles from the camp – before dispatching the gringo to his Maker.

Luke had left his saddle-bag with his books in it with Paco, except for the copy of *Don Quixote* which he had kept with him. He had told Paco that if they weren't back by the end of the month he should sell the books, and give the regulars in the cantina a drink on him. The only things that he had kept from the saddle-bag were a change of underwear and a pair of guns. Velarde's eyes widened as he watched Luke strapping on his guns. He was a knife man himself, but he could recognize a pair of guns that had been polished and oiled ready for action. Luke made quite a show of strapping on the guns, aware that Velarde was watching him with more than a little apprehension.

'See these,' said Luke, as he flicked the bullets into their chambers.

Velarde nodded.

'One of them is for you, if you try to double-cross me. *Comprende?*'

Velarde decided that he would have to treat the American with more respect than he had at first assumed.

They had a couple of hours of daylight left before sunset. Velarde's mule obediently trotted alongside the white horse. Perhaps he had sensed that he was going home, Luke decided, inwardly pleased with the fact that the mule was not slowing them down.

No conversation passed between them. Luke had no idea what he was going to do when he reached the camp. Assuming, that was, he reached the camp alive, since Velarde would obviously make his play some distance from the camp. His objective would be to bring Luke's corpse into the camp. He would immediately be proclaimed the bandidos' hero. Velarde would be wined and dined and fêted.

Luke decided to forget about what was going to happen when he reached the camp. He would let events take their course. His first priority was to ensure that he stayed alive so that he could make an attempt at rescuing Maria.

The sun was getting lower on the hilltops. Another half an hour and they would have to camp down for the night. Since they had left the town the only person they had met was a peon in charge of a rickety cart. He glanced curiously at the two as they approached, but made no effort to greet them. Velarde's face was enough to make anyone who was thinking of greeting them change their minds, Luke surmised.

When they were making camp for the night Luke broke the silence. 'Why were you hiding in Paco's cellar?' he demanded.

'Paco is my cousin,' Velarde replied. 'He knew that Ricardo would kill me for not killing you. So he said I could use his cellar to hide in, until I thought it was safe to come out.'

Luke had always trusted Paco. He had assumed he was that rarity, an honest Mexican. But now it looked as though Paco had helped to set him up. When Velarde had attacked him, Paco must have passed the word to him that then was an opportune moment. Luke sighed. That was another of his illusions shattered, that Paco was a trustworthy citizen. As they used to say in the cavalry, never trust a Mex. It looked as though it had been good advice.

Chapter 7

The next two days passed uneventfully. They were riding through a semi-desert. After mid-morning the sun beat down mercilessly on them. At first Luke amused himself by identifying any plants that they came across. There were octillos, creosote bushes and mesquites. Soon, however, they ran out of plants as the desert took over. Anyhow, Luke was soon unable to play the game any longer since all he could think about was the searing heat as they plodded on.

Not one word was spoken between them, although from time to time Velarde would glance at him. Luke wondered whether the bandit was checking to see whether he was alive and well, so that he could have the pleasure of killing him and bringing in Luke's corpse to the camp.

57

Only in the evenings when the sun was low in the sky could Luke's addled brain begin to function normally. The doubts which he had harboured during the day would begin to melt away. He would begin to picture Maria's lovely face again. It gave him the added resolve to carry on.

At the end of the second day Luke was presented with a problem. After eating his meagre supper of bread and water, he knew that he soon had to decide whether he could chance things and go to sleep. Paco had said it would take two or three days to reach the bandits' camp. It meant that they should reach the camp tomorrow. So there was a distinct probability that Velarde would make his move tonight.

Luke sighed. It seemed that he had no choice. Although he was dead tired after spending eight hours in the saddle, he would have to stay awake, or he wouldn't see another dawn.

He took up his usual position about a hundred feet from Velarde. Luke had reasoned on the first night that he had wanted as much space between them as was possible without raising Velarde's suspicions. Another consideration was that Velarde smelled. Luke, who had always been particular about his personal cleanliness, knew that he, too, was beginning to smell. But since there hadn't been any sign of any streams in the baked desert through which they had been riding, he hadn't been able even to wash his face. The water that they had been carrying was so precious that they had to save every drop.

Luke stretched out and covered himself with his two blankets as usual. Although the heat was scorching in the daytime, the temperature dropped alarmingly at night, and the two blankets were essential. In spite of that Luke had noted that Velarde would lie down on the ground without the luxury of any blankets. Another advantage of the blankets was that Luke was able to hide a gun between them. It would be out of sight to an approaching Velarde.

To try to keep awake Luke began reciting poetry to himself. He recited poems by his favourite poets, Byron, Keats and Shelley. When he had exhausted all the ones he could remember he began on Shakespeare. He knew at least two of the plays almost word for word since he had taken part in amateur productions when in school. In *The Tempest* he had taken the part of Prospero, partly because he was almost a foot taller than other boys in his class, and so presented a commanding figure. He had got through the first four acts and was just beginning Prospero's famous speech:

Ye elves of hills, brooks, standing lakes
    and groves;
And ye that on the sand with printless
    foot do chase the ebbing Neptune,
And do flee him when he comes back . . .

when Velarde made his move. He covered the distance between them with the speed of a mountain leopard. In fact he moved so quickly that he almost took Luke by surprise. Velarde sprang on him and Luke had no time to pull his gun out from its hiding place before he was struggling with his attacker.

The raised knife had gleamed in the faint moonlight and Luke was just in time to roll to one side and avoid its downward thrust. Soon they were grunting as they struggled to gain the upper hand. They had rolled free of the blankets and although the gun was only a foot away it might as well have been in San Caldiz for all the use it would be to him now. A line of poetry of one of Luke's other favourite poets flashed through his mind as he held Velarde's arms aloft; 'The best-laid schemes o' mice and men . . .'

Luke knew that he was stronger than Velarde, but the Mex was a slippery customer. Once Luke had let him out of his grasp he would gather his resources for one more spring. Maybe next time the Mex would be luckier and his knife would find its target. Luke knew as they rolled over and over that he had to hold on to the potentially lethal knife hand at all costs.

The progress of their death dance was suddenly arrested by a rock. It had been one of the reasons why they had decided to camp there for the night – a couple of the rocks had seemed more hospitable than just camping in the middle of the desert. Now there was no way of escape for Velarde. Luke knew that the odds had definitely swung in his favour. All he had to do was to take the knife from him.

The Mex hung on to it grimly. It was the weapon which was to have been his salvation. Now the accursed gringo was showing every sign of taking it from him. He began to swear desperately.

Luke began to prise one of Velarde's fingers off the knife. He knew from previous brawls when in the cavalry that the finger to choose was the little finger. Without it the Mex's downward thrust would be virtually useless. Luke began to force it back pitilessly.

Velarde gave a final scream before his finger broke. The knife dropped from his hand. Luke scooped it up. He sucked in huge gulps of breath as he slowly dragged his weary body towards his blankets.

Velarde was whimpering where Luke had left him. Luke fetched out the gun and returned the few yards to the rock. At his approach the Mex stopped whimpering. He eyed the gun fatalistically. 'Go on, shoot me,' he said, defiantly. 'I'm no good to anyone now.'

Luke couldn't help but admire the tattered shred of dignity which Velarde had dragged up from somewhere in the depths of his personality. 'How far away are we from camp?' he demanded.

'Two hours,' said Velarde, sullenly.

'Right, then as soon as it's sun-up we ride into the camp. Try to keep your hand still until then. You'll find the old women in the camp will know all about knit-bone. They've probably been using it for generations. One of them will fix your hand up and it will be as good as new.'

'Some use it will be to me when I'm dead,' said Velarde, glumly. 'When Ricardo finds out that I have let you escape twice, my life won't be worth half a peseta.'

'I think we can get around that problem,' said

Luke. He began to explain his plan. When he had finished, Velarde, although in considerable pain, managed a twisted smile.

Chapter 8

Around mid-day two figures rode into the Mexican camp. Luke was uncomfortably aware of the twin rows of guns that followed their progress. They were like a bride and groom going down the aisle, he thought, humorously. Only the guests were the bandits' guns.

They were heading slowly towards a large man who had been seated, Indian-fashion, among a group of bandits, but who had now risen to greet them. This was Ricardo, the one whom Luke had seen carry Maria away. Luke clenched his hands so tightly in frustration that his finger nails scored into his hands. Outwardly he smiled at Ricardo.

Velarde dropped down from his mule and Luke dismounted from his horse. He knew that one false move, one wrong statement even, and, at a command from Ricardo, the rows of bandits with the waiting rifles would open fire, and he would never see Maria again. At least not on this earth.

He smiled falsely as he approached Ricardo. Like many male Mexicans the bandit leader equated virility with the ability to grow a large moustache. If the theory were true Ricardo should have dozens of children by this time. The large moustache curled not once, but twice. Its waxed ends were perfectly in position on his rather large reddish face.

'I see you've brought your prisoner in, Velarde,' said Ricardo, sarcastically.

'He wishes to discuss a matter of business with you, Ricardo,' said Velarde, nervously.

'In that case you had better come into my tent,' said Ricardo. 'But first I must insist on having your guns. My *bandidos* have itchy fingers and if you should make the wrong move while still carrying your guns, they might begin to scratch.' He roared at the joke. The couple of dozen or so *bandidos* who had been following Luke's progress with avid eyes, waiting for that decisive moment when Luke would go for his guns, almost gave a collective sigh of disappointment as they watched him take off his gun belt and hand it to Ricardo. 'I'll have Velarde's knife as well,' added the outlaw.

Luke realized he was up against a clever man as he drew Velarde's knife out of his boot and handed it over.

'Right,' said Ricardo, turning to lead the way into the large tent. 'Welcome to my humble abode.'

When they were seated in the tent Ricardo waited until one of the boys had brought in a bottle of tequila and some glasses before starting the discussion. Ricardo spent the few moments studying Luke intently like a portrait painter trying to decide how much of a certain colour to use on the portrait of his favourite sitter. Although Luke tried to remain impassive under the constant gaze, he knew that he was sweating profusely.

There were three others in the tent. Two of them were obviously Ricardo's bodyguards – their status underlined by the guns which they held at the ready. Velarde was the third. If Luke thought that he was feeling uncomfortable in the present situation, Velarde looked as though he was slowly disintegrating. He was wiping his face every few seconds with a grubby handkerchief. The fact that Ricardo glanced at him and shook his head pityingly gave him no cause to raise his hopes.

The drinks finally arrived. There were generous quantities in the tall glasses. Luke accepted his and raised his glass to Ricardo. The bandit responded with a thin smile and raised his glass in return. Velarde grabbed his drink thankfully and swallowed it, spilling some of it in his eagerness to down it.

'Now, let's get down to business,' said Ricardo.

'I brought him in, as you ordered,' cut in Velarde quickly.

Ricardo ignored him. 'What have you got to say?' demanded the bandit leader.

Luke took another pull at his drink.. He knew that his life was hanging on a thin thread. If he made a mistake during the next few minutes that thread would surely snap. And any hope he had of finally rescuing Maria would certainly disappear.

'I took the post with your brother,' he began, 'pretending to be a teacher. I was working with the person in charge of supplying morphine to the Third United States Cavalry in Fort Manton.'

'What's his name?' demanded Ricardo, impassively.

'Carl Pinard,' supplied Luke.

Ricardo nodded almost imperceptibly.

First hurdle over, thought Luke. Only about a dozen to go. 'Carl said that Garcia was the front man in a large organization south of the border. My job was to try to get in contact with him, so that he could supply morphine to the Third Cavalry. I don't know whether you know it, but over half the soldiers are on the drug. They can't get enough of it.'

Ricardo smiled his thin smile. Luke could see that the bandit leader was interested. He took another sip of the tequila. He was beginning to relax for the first time since entering the tent. 'So I took the post of tutor to Garcia's children. I had to take a genuine job so as not to arouse suspicions. I found however that Garcia had broken off his connection with supplying the drugs.' Luke prayed that his guess was right.

Ricardo's brow darkened. 'The cheating dog double-crossed me,' he stormed. 'I had been supplying the drugs to him and he had been shipping them across the border. Then suddenly – do you know what he tells me?'

Luke shook his head.

'He tells me the whole operation is finished. He has become too respectable to be a drug-dealer. He has made enough money out of it – money which I made for him – and now he wants to quit. I argue with him. I give him time to change his mind. After all, we are brothers, we do not behave like uncivilized Indians. I tell him I know we have made plenty of money, but there is plenty more where that came from. Finally I give him time to reconsider.'

'Thirty days,' supplied Luke.

'You know everything, don't you?' snarled Ricardo.

It had been a reasonable guess. Luke remembered Ricardo coming to the villa. After his departure it had seemed as if there was a dark cloud hanging over it. Without anyone knowing exactly what was going on it was obvious to the staff that something was brewing. Even Luke and his pupils were affected by the depression which seemed to pervade everything. To escape from the gloom Luke would often in the evenings take Maria for a walk. And that was when he had fallen in love with her, he now realized with sudden certainty.

'He didn't change his mind, so I killed him,' said Ricardo flatly.

Luke took another pull at his tequila. So much for brotherly love, he thought. He really was getting a taste for the tequila. It seemed sweeter than the usual mule's piss that Paco served.

'How much morphine does Carl Pinard want?' demanded Ricardo.

Luke pulled a quantity out of the air. 'A hundred pounds,' he replied.

Ricardo did not bat an eyelid. It was funny though how his own eyelids seemed to be getting heavy. He let one drop and it didn't want to get back up again. Then suddenly the tent started swaying. He had never known a tent sway like this before, not even in a high wind. The realization that his drink had been drugged hit him at the same time as he fell from his chair.

Chapter 9

Half an hour later there were three men in
Ricardo's tent: Ricardo himself, and the other
two whom Luke had assumed were bodyguards
but were actually the *jefe*'s trusted lieutenants.
Luke himself had been moved to another tent to
sleep off his drugged condition. There was no
guard on the tent, Ricardo having reasoned that
since Luke had come all this way to hope to go
into business with him, then he shouldn't need a
guard. However, as a precaution, Ricardo told
the two men who had carried Luke to the tent to
take away Luke's trousers, leaving him only in
his long-johns.

'So what do we do?' asked one lieutenant,
whose name was Pedro. He was stocky, swarthy,
with jet-black curly hair, and a wide smile. If

Ricardo had asked him he would willingly have killed Luke and the smile would still have been on his face.

'Yes, what do you think we should do?' echoed the other, whose name was Arturo. He was tall and thin with a perpetual lugubrious expression on his face.

Ricardo didn't answer immediately. Instead he examined a silver-coloured eight-pointed star which he held in his hand. Finally he said, 'This belongs to Ballard. We found it in his trouser pocket. It's the cap badge of the Third Cavalry. It's the proof we needed that he really was in the Cavalry. Do you know, in the wars with the Indians some of the Indian tribes were afraid of the Cavalry, not so much because of their guns but because they thought these stars held some magic powers. The Cavalry had won their battle almost before they had began shooting.'

Pedro grinned at the anecdote and Arturo acknowledged it with a wry smile. 'Right, let's get down to business,' stated Ricardo, tossing the star aside.

'So we believe the gringo's story,' stated Pedro.

'I didn't say that,' said Ricardo, sharply. 'All we can say is that he was definitely in the Cavalry. Whether he has come here to set up a deal for

our opium or whether he has come here for
another purpose is for us to find out.'

'For what purpose could he have come here?'
demanded Arturo.

'He could be a spy for the United States
Government,' stated Ricardo, flatly.

The others took in the implication. Ricardo
took a pull at his glass of tequila.

'Why should they send a spy here?' demanded
Pedro, finally.

'Surely it's obvious,' snapped Ricardo. 'The
United States has always been against our
opium business. They are ruled by a lot of bible-
punchers who don't take any notice of what the
ordinary people want. The same thing happened
in Britain when they found that the East India
Company was making most of its money out of
opium and not tea as everyone had thought.' He
smiled at the deception. 'Now somehow or other
we've got to find out whether Ballard is genuine
or not.'

'But even if he is a spy,' stated Arturo, 'what
harm could he do us? We are not under the
United States Government, we are under the
Mexican Government. We pay a share of the
profits to the President. He is getting hundreds
of thousands of *dineros* every year without even

having to send a taxman round. Everybody is
happy. So why should the United States want to
get mixed up in our own country's arrangements?'

'If the United States feels that its Cavalry is
not winning enough battles against the Indians
because its soldiers are already on cloud nine
through using our opium, they'll argue that
they've got every right to try to put a halt to
their supplies,' retorted Ricardo.

The other two digested the implication
thoughtfully. Finally Pedro said, 'How are we
going to find out whether he's a spy or not?
Torture him?'

'It may come to that,' said Ricardo, coldly. 'But
if we do and we find that he's genuine, we may
have physically damaged an ally. No, we'll use
that dancing girl, what's her name?'

'Rosita,' supplied Pedro.

'We'll use Rosita to get friendly with him. I
heard they were quite friendly when they were
in my brother's villa. Go and fetch her, Pedro.' As
Pedro was about to leave the tent, Ricardo
stopped him. 'Wait, I've got a better idea. We'll
have a barbecue. Food and wine for everyone.
Rosita can dance for the gringo. Afterwards he
can take her back to his tent. Her task will be to

find out whether he is a genuine go-between for the Cavalry and us. By tomorrow we should know one way or the other.'

Chapter 10

When Luke awoke it was to the pleasant sensation that someone was wiping his brow. He opened his eyes. There were two young Mexican girls in his tent. They both had jet-black hair, large eyes and flawless light brown skin and were just at the age to start turning men's heads. One was mopping his brow, which was the cause of the pleasant sensation on Luke's forehead, while the other was holding the bowl.

When they saw that Luke was awake they gave squeals of surprise. The one almost dropped the bowl, while the other did succeed in dropping the cloth, with the result that Luke received a more than half damp cloth smack in his face.

They were full of remorse and apologies. 'Don't worry,' said Luke, with a half smile. 'There's been no harm done.'

'You speak Spanish?' said one, wonderingly.

'In the outside world,' Luke assured them, 'there are lots of gringos who can speak Spanish.'

He found out that their names were Teresa and Anna and that they had been commanded by Ricardo to tend to his wishes. After checking that he was no worse for being drugged, Luke asked them to bring him some soap and a razor.

They watched him while he shaved, their luminous eyes following every movement he made.

'How old are you?' demanded Luke.

'I'm Teresa. I'm twelve. Anna's thirteen,' one responded. It was the opportunity which they had been waiting for to begin chattering. They told him about their cousin, Marguerette, who was thirteen, who was getting married the following week. As Luke had guessed they were sisters and each of them would soon be 'promised' to a man in the camp. Rapport having been established, Luke ventured a question which he had been aching to ask ever since he had arrived in the camp.

'I understand that Ricardo's niece, Maria, is going to get married soon.'

Suddenly their expressions became frozen with fear. Where they had been like chattering

monkeys, they now became sullen and silent. It
didn't take a genius to work out that Luke had
said the wrong thing.

He tried to coax them out of their silence while
he washed, but a wall of silence had descended
between them. Finally Luke's ablutions were
complete. He felt physically refreshed. He was
thinking about a way of making them talk when
Velarde arrived on the scene. The girls packed up
with alacrity and left.

Velarde's hand was bandaged and Luke
enquired about it solicitously. Velarde held it up
proudly as though it were a trophy. 'A couple of
the ladies did me the favour of fixing it for me,'
he stated. 'Afterwards, I did them both a favour,'
he boasted.

'So all's well that ends well,' observed Luke.

'You could say that,' stated Velarde.

'To what do I owe the honour of this visit?'
demanded Luke.

'You are the one who is to be honoured,'
retorted Velarde, drawing out a couple of thin
cigars from a packet and handing one to Luke.

Luke accepted it. He waited until they were
both ignited before asking, 'What exactly do you
mean?'

'They're going to have a barbecue this evening

81

in your honour. There'll be wine, women and song.' His eyes shone at the prospect.

'I'd have thought that you'd have had enough women already,' remarked Luke, drily.

'You don't understand,' retorted Velarde. 'With my appearance it is hard to attract women, unless I pay for them. And then the ones I have would be out of the gutter. But today I have had two beautiful women with beautiful bodies. And why? Because you are my friend. We came into camp together. I have helped Ricardo arrange a meeting which will help him to sell more opium. The more opium he can sell, the happier everyone in the camp is. And that is why Ricardo will be holding a barbecue soon. To show that everybody is happy.'

'What about Maria Garcia? Is she happy?' snapped Luke.

Velarde shrugged. 'I do not know anything about her. Except that they say they are keeping her drugged until the *padre* arrives. But why do you concern yourself about her? She is going to marry Paulo. You must not have eyes for her. You can have anyone you like tonight. You can have the two young girls who were here. They are pretty, and I believe that one of them is still a virgin. . . .'

'All right, that's enough,' snapped Luke. 'Out you go. Go on – vamoose.'

Velarde accepted his dismissal with equanimity. 'I'll see you at the barbecue,' he stated, as he left the tent.

Chapter 11

Rosita was dancing and the audience were clapping to the rhythm of her dance. Luke, as befitting the guest of honour, was seated next to Ricardo. The evening sun was casting long shadows over the camp and it was pleasant to relax with a glass of tequila (this time not drugged, Ricardo had assured him with a smile) and watch Rosita's sinuous movements.

There was a sense of déjà vu about the whole scene thought Luke. Except that this time there was no villa in the background, only the tents of the bandits. Also, although there were Mexicans standing around with their carbines, this time, as far as he knew, there would be no shooting.

Luke had had his first glimpse of Maria about ten minutes before, and he had been shocked by

what he had seen. She had entered the
makeshift auditorium supported by two middle-
aged ladies. Her 'ladies-in-waiting' thought Luke
humorously, as he had watched their slow
progress to their seats. Velarde had prepared
him for the fact that she had been drugged, but
the way she had had to be supported suggested
that they must have pumped a large quantity
into her. They came towards his seat and when
they were about to pass it, Luke expected a sign
of recognition from Maria, but she only gave him
a cursory glance before continuing with her slow
progress.

It was probably better for their safety that she
hadn't given him a welcoming smile, conceded
Luke. He knew that Ricardo was watching him
like a hawk. Any false move which didn't fit the
image he had tried to create would be seized
upon, chewed over, digested, and then he would
be called to account for it. If his explanation was
unsatisfactory, he knew with a burning certainty
that he could end up being buried alive in the
ant pit. So although he was sick in his stomach
at the treatment being meted out to Maria, for
the moment at least, it was for the better.

There was no doubt that Rosita was dancing
for him. She approached as closely as she dared,

almost brushing him with her twirling skirt. She smiled at him coquettishly, then hid her face behind her fan. Her body swayed like a cobra in front of him. Her lips were slightly parted and she licked them suggestively. Luke hated being the centre of attention, but there was nothing he could do, except stare at her, hypnotized, as she moved around him. He couldn't help but remember the time they had spent together under the trees. It had been a night of madness, he told himself, savagely. It had all been in the past. His true love was seated about a hundred yards away, with the two women.

The dance finally finished. Rosita flung herself into Luke's arms and he was forced to catch her. There was an enthusiastic applause all round the camp. Rosita smiled delightedly up at Luke. Then she reached up, pulled his head down, and kissed him.

'I think you're going to be busy for the next hour,' said Ricardo, with a wide grin.

To Luke's dismay Rosita insisted on being carried to his tent. He carried her victoriously like a Greek warrior who had just vanquished his lover and was now claiming his just rewards. They were forced to pass Maria, who seemed to be watching their progress through befuddled eyes. With a bit of luck, thought Luke, Maria was too drugged to realize what was going on.

Inside the tent it was obvious that Rosita was not going to waste any time. She had already kicked off her boots and began to strip off her blouse. When she had undone the last buttons she tossed it on the floor. The fullness of her breasts with their proud nipples were revealed and Luke eyed them with a mixture of trepidation and desire. She began to unwind a cummerbund from around her waist.

The garment was soon fully detached from Rosita's body and she turned her attention to her skirt.

Rosita whipped off her brightly coloured skirt triumphantly. For a few seconds she held it aloft like a bull fighter flourishing his cape. Then there was only Rosita's flame coloured knickers left. She lay back on the bed. In the semi-darkness Luke thought that her eyes had narrowed. Her hands were behind her head in an attitude of supplication. Suddenly the flap of the tent was forced open and a voice bellowed, 'What do you think you are doing with my wife?'

A stocky Mexican was standing there. He held an angry-looking gun in his hand.

'Go away, Stephano!' hissed Rosita.

'Not before I've killed this gringo first,' insisted Stephano.

'I didn't know you were married,' claimed Luke. The statement fell on deaf ears as Rosita and Stephano were glaring with hatred at each other. An interested knot of spectators had gathered outside the tent. Rosita, suddenly aware of her nakedness, began to put her clothes back on with startling rapidity. With such rapidity in fact that Luke couldn't help wondering how often she had been in similar situations before.

Luke stepped outside the tent. 'You'd better see Ricardo,' he told Stephano. 'He can explain everything.'

The gun showed no sign of wavering. 'It's you I've come to see, gringo,' said Stephano. 'You can either fight like a man or die like a coward. You can choose which way you want to die.'

The crowd was growing bigger by the second. 'You can't fight him,' a now fully dressed Rosita pleaded with Luke. 'He's killed dozens of men.'

'At the moment, as you can see,' Luke held his arms wide to emphasize the point, 'I haven't any guns.'

'That can easily be changed,' said a third voice. It was Ricardo, who advanced towards them.

'You want me to fight him?' said a surprised Luke.

'Why not? It is a matter of honour. Every man must fight for his honour.'

'But I've got no quarrel against this man,' protested Luke.

'He's got a quarrel against you,' Ricardo pointed out.

'It's a misunderstanding. I didn't know he was married to Rosita.' Luke looked around in order for her to confirm his error. But she was nowhere to be seen.

'I'm ready to start,' said Stephano, with an insistence that Luke was beginning to find wearing.

'He says he hasn't got any quarrel with you,' said Ricardo.

Stephano's answer was to point his pistol at Luke's feet and pull the trigger. Luke was forced to jump in the air like a startled jack-rabbit again and again. The crowd of spectators roared with laughter. When Stephano had emptied the chamber of his gun and the amusement of the crowd had subsided Ricardo looked at Luke's hard face.

'He's got a quarrel now,' he stated, positively.

One of Ricardo's assistants brought an exquisite pair of pearl-handled guns. 'For you,' he stated.

'I want my own guns,' insisted Luke.

'But *señor*, these are perfect. . . .'

'My own guns, or I won't fight,' snapped Luke.

'Fetch them,' ordered Ricardo, with displeasure in his voice.

The assembled spectators began to place bets. Velarde appeared on the scene. 'I will be your second,' he said. 'To see that everything is fair and square.' He offered Luke a cigar, an offer which was refused. 'Maybe you're right,' agreed Velarde. 'I'll keep one until after the duel.'

Luke noticed that most of the bets seemed to be going on his opponent. Luke's guns arrived. He examined them. Except for being a bit dusty they seemed in perfect condition. He called for a duster and carefully cleaned them. Velarde watched him as he polished them.

'Two things I learned in the Cavalry,' Luke informed him. 'Polish your guns and polish your boots. By the way,' he added. 'Have you put a bet on me winning?' He could tell by his second's sheepish expression that he had put his money on Stephano. 'Oh, ye of little faith,' Luke quoted, as he took up his position as instructed by Ricardo.

Luke noticed that the low sun was to his right and therefore would make no difference to his taking aim. On the other hand, Stephano would be at a slight disadvantage, since he would catch sight of the sun out of the corner of his eye, and that distraction could possibly prove fatal. Luke guessed that they were about forty feet apart. He would have preferred another ten feet, since at forty feet, he could easily get killed by a badly aimed bullet. But the decision wasn't his, so he had to accept it.

'Aim!' Ricardo barked out the command.

Luke was ice-cool. He might have been aiming in the practice ground in the cavalry yard. He aimed directly between his opponent's eyes, then allowed for deviation, as his instructor had taught him. He knew he had to make the first bullet count. He might not have a chance of a second.

'Fire!' yelled Ricardo.

Chapter 12

Maria was vaguely aware that something exciting was happening. The two ladies who had been assigned to look after her, Camilla and Penelope, conveyed this excitement by leaving her from time to time. They would take it in turns to leave her side, one hurrying back as the other disappeared for a short while. Before that she had recognized a familiar sound, that of rhythmic clapping. It had made her want to join in. But it was as if her arms and hands didn't want to obey her brain. Anyhow there was so much sheep's wool around her brain that she couldn't make sense out of anything.

Most of the time she had managed to avoid taking the drug, hoping to keep a clear head. But this morning there had been no escape from the persistence of Camilla and Penelope, and she had been forced to take a spoonful of the opaque liquid.

She wished she could remember something. Anything, so that she could try to concentrate on it. It was as if her concentration had vanished. She was no longer able to picture things in her mind and hang on to that picture. Her mind kept playing tricks on her. Even when she recognized a face she couldn't remember who the person was. There was that man they had passed when they had arrived at their seat. She could have sworn she knew him from somewhere. But where? He had looked at her as if he recognized her. But who was he? Where had she seen him before. It seemed vitally important that she remembered. But, try as she could, she didn't succeed.

When Camilla and Penelope dashed in with the news that there was going to be a fight, she hardly took any notice of the announcement. It was nothing to do with her. She had always been kept away from fights. In the mission school which she had attended, there were high walls which protected her from fights. It was funny, the way she could picture the mission school, yet she couldn't bring to mind any of the daily events which had happened to her since then.

Both of her companions went outside to watch the fight. Perhaps she should go out, too. She had never seen a fight and so perhaps now was the time to begin. After all, she was a big girl now. She didn't need to be mollycoddled any more. She didn't need to be protected. Yes, she'd go out and watch the fight as well.

Her companions were surprised when she staggered out of the tent. They ran forward and caught her before she fell. They had an argument about whether to put her back inside the tent. During the argument she stood between them swaying and they supported her on either side. Finally they agreed to let her watch the fight. As Penelope said, 'It doesn't matter if she watches it. She won't understand anything about it.'

They put her in a chair where she could watch the two gunmen. Although she didn't know the cause of the fight she guessed that one of them was going to kill the other. She wondered vaguely which one was going to win, the stocky one or the tall one? Wait a minute, there was something vaguely familiar about the tall one. She was sure that she had seen him before. But where?

She focused her entire attention on him. It seemed a matter of life or death for her to be able to remember where they had met before. She watched with agitation as the two men stood the required distance apart. Her companions regarded her disturbed state with amusement. She tried to stand, but they held on to her firmly. Her head was shaking as she tried to recollect the name of the gunfighter. All eyes were fixed on the scene which was being played out in the hollow below. Ricardo began to count. A hush had descended as the watchers held their breath. Maria knew that on the count of 'three' one of them was going to be killed. Suddenly she found herself praying that it wouldn't be the tall American. It was the first time that she had succeeded in praying for days. Tears rolled down her face, but her companions were too busy waiting for the count of three to notice.

'Three!' screamed Ricardo. The two shots seemed to come simultaneously. For a second both men stood there. Then the Mexican slowly collapsed. All eyes were fixed on the American who was still standing.

'Luke!' cried Maria, and fainted.

Chapter 13

Luke was being attended in his tent by Teresa and Anna. They giggled and chattered as they tended his wound. They were cutting a strip of cloth to wrap round his wounded hand.

'Does it hurt?' asked Anna, the more serious of the two.

'Only when I use it to smack you on your bottom,' he retorted.

The remark sent them into peals of laughter. Finally Anna said, 'Now, hold still while I wrap this round your hand.'

Luke obligingly held his hand still. He was still feeling light-headed after emerging the winner in the duel. He knew he would be playing the scene in his mind over and over during the next few days. Ricardo counting three. The sounds of the guns which merged into one. The tug at his left hand which had told him that Stephano's shot was hopelessly wide. The hole which had appeared in the middle of Stephano's forehead, followed by his slow collapse.

He had had no compunctions about killing Stephano. Rosita's husband had called him, and that was that. He had given him a couple of chances to change his mind, but Stephano had refused. So it had either been his own death, or Stephano's. It was as simple as that.

The chattering girls had mentioned Maria's name. It jerked Luke out of his reverie.

'What did you say?' he demanded.

'I said she fainted when she saw your blood,' said Teresa.

'I don't know what's to faint about,' said Anna. 'It looks ordinary blood to me.' They went into paroxysms of laughter.

So Maria had watched the duel. And what she had seen had caused her to faint. It might mean something, he thought, hopefully, as he tested whether they had tied the bandage too tightly or not.

Ricardo entered and the girls made themselves scarce. 'I see you had a slight wound,' he said, seating himself on the only stool in the tent.

'It was nothing,' said Luke.

'That's good,' said Ricardo, 'because tomorrow I'll take you to the poppy-fields. You'll see how our organization works.'

'I can't wait,' replied Luke.

Ricardo eyed him suspiciously, as though there might be some hidden meaning behind the remark. Then suddenly his face changed. It split into one of his enormous grins. He began to roar with laughter. 'I think we will make a great team, eh, gringo?' he said. He was still chuckling as he left the tent.

Luke had two more visitors before he was allowed to take a well-deserved rest.

The first was Velarde, who was obviously delighted with Luke's victory. 'What a duel! What a shot! Right between the eyes,' he enthused.

'I just hope there aren't any other jealous husbands going to challenge me,' stated Luke, as he accepted the inevitable cigar.

'I should think Ricardo should be pleased with your killing,' stated the other.

'What's Ricardo got to do with it?' demanded Luke.

'Don't you know?' asked an astonished Velarde. 'Ricardo arranged everything. He kept

99

telling Stephano how you were having an affair with Rosita when you were both at his brother's villa. He built Stephano up into a state of jealous rage. That's why Stephano challenged you to a duel. Now Ricardo has got a clear field with Rosita. He's clever, isn't he?'

Not so clever that one day he won't be able to avoid me killing him, thought Luke viciously, as he took a long draw at his cigar.

Luke was on the point of having a deserved rest when his other visitor appeared. To his surprise it was Zapote.

'What brings you to this part of the world?' asked Luke, drily.

'I'll say this quickly,' said Zapote, 'because it will seem suspicious if I stay here for long. Can I trust you?'

'I hope so,' said Luke. 'What's behind the question?'

'I suppose I've no choice,' said Zapote, half to himself.

'Are you going to tell me what this is all about?' demanded Luke, impatiently. 'I've had a tiring day, and now I intend getting some sleep.'

'I'm a government agent,' said Zapote, quickly. 'I've been sent here to find out about the opium operation which Ricardo is controlling.'

'I wish you luck,' said Luke. 'Now if you please leave my tent, I propose to get some sleep.'

'I've come to propose a deal,' said Zapote. 'You help me to get information about the poppy-fields . . .'

'And what do I get in return?'

'I help you to get Maria back to civilization before they drug her so much that she will become ruined for life.'

Chapter 14

Ricardo called early to take Luke to the poppy-fields. 'As they say in English, it's the early worm that catches the bird,' he laughed, uproariously.

Luke did not bother to correct him. In the first place he disliked people who were full of *joie-de-vivre* first thing in the morning. In the second place he hated Ricardo with a burning hatred which he only hoped wouldn't be too obvious as they rode out of the camp.

Ricardo was accompanied by his two lieutenants, Arturo and Pedro. All four were silent as they headed towards the low hills. Normally this would have been the best time of the day to ride. The sun was still blanketed in a low mist and the air still held the night chill which made it invigorating and filled one with anticipation of the day ahead. In normal circumstances, Luke supposed he would have enjoyed the ride. But these weren't normal circumstances – he was going to view the place where human misery was created on a huge scale. He had seen how heroin addiction had affected ordinary, decent, soldiers. He had seen how the craving for the drug had taken over their lives – how they could think of nothing else but getting their next supply of the drug.

They had been riding for about half an hour when Ricardo suddenly pulled up. He pointed to a valley ahead. 'We're almost there,' he announced.

Sure enough Luke could soon see the poppy-fields. They stretched as far as the eye could see. White carpets of poppies stood in stark contrast to the light brown of the soil. Ricardo kept glancing at Luke to see whether he was impressed. If they had been fields of any other flower except the opium poppy he would have been overawed by the mass of colour which lay ahead.

'You have never seen anything like it?' demanded Ricardo, seeking verification of the unique scene.

'No, never,' admitted Luke, truthfully.

'We have three streams running down into the

fields,' said Ricardo, proudly. 'So the ground is never completely dry.'

They were now riding in the middle of the carpet of poppies. Luke could see that ahead they were being picked by women pickers. Ricardo drew up his horse and the others followed suit.

'We pick the poppies at this time of the year,' he announced. 'As you can see the women pick them.'

There were about fifty women stretched out in a line across the field in front of them. They were all bent double, picking the flowers and putting them in what appeared to be a huge pocket in the front of the smock they were wearing. Ricardo dismounted and the others did the same. Some boys appeared to take their horses. Ricardo began to walk towards the pickers.

'They can pick like this from dawn to dusk,' he informed Luke, 'without stopping,' he added.

Luke had read about slave labour, but surely this compared with anything he had read about how the negroes had been forced to work in the cotton-fields. Ricardo pointed to several men who were standing on the edge of the field. They had wicked looking whips in their hands. 'If the women get tired, then they will remind them to get on with their work.'

They were walking towards some low sheds where Luke had guessed the flowers were stored. When they arrived there the guard stepped reverently aside. They entered one of the sheds.

'The flowers are stored here while they are drying,' explained Ricardo. Luke took in the rows upon rows of wide shelves which were covered with the heads of the flowers. 'It takes hundreds of flowers just to get a few ounces of opium,' he continued.

'How do you crush the flowers?' demanded Luke.

'I'm coming to that,' announced Ricardo. He led the way into a shed at the end. This, too, was guarded by an armed guard. Ricardo waved him aside and they entered the shed.

There were sacks of poppies stacked at one end waiting to be crushed. Pride of place belonged to the crusher which stood on a low table in the middle of the floor. A man was operating it and Ricardo tapped him on the shoulder to cease his activities.

The crusher was a comparatively small machine. It was like a football with knives which entered holes to slice the poppy-capsules when the handle was turned. The crusher took the capsules and then crushed them into the thick colourless liquid which was slowly coming out of the funnel as the operator turned the handle. This was then collected into the rows of bottles which stood on a shelf. Later, with the use of a hypodermic needle the opium would be transferred into a person's vein, and it would begin to work its evil – gradually taking control of the person's body, and eventually his mind. Of course, as morphine it had helped to alleviate suffering and save lives, particularly during the civil war. He had heard tales in the mess-room of how, at the beginning of the war, men had been forced to have limbs amputated without the use of anaesthetic – before the hypodermic had been invented. But towards the end of the war, when it became available, its use had saved countless soldiers from hours of agony.

When they were back out in the open, Ricardo said, 'Impressive, eh?'

Despite his misgivings about the major use to which the opium was going to be put, Luke had to admit it was.

'Tomorrow you will go back to Fort Manton. You will tell Major Pinard what you've seen. You'll arrange for us to supply the fort with opium. You will be well rewarded.'

Back in his tent, Luke was thinking how he could get out of the tricky situation, when he had a visitor. It was Zapote. Luke's greeting was cool, but Zapote ignored it and went straight down to business. 'I believe you visited the poppy-fields this morning,' he stated.

Luke nodded.

'I want you to give me an exact description of what you saw. It could be vital to my plan.'

Luke saw no reason for not complying. After all, hadn't Zapote promised that he would help him to rescue Maria. Although for the life of him at the moment he couldn't see the remotest possibility of achieving this.

When he had finished bringing Zapote up to date about his visit to the poppy-fields, the Mexican beamed with satisfaction. 'Good!' he exclaimed.

'I'm supposed to be going to Fort Manton tomorrow to arrange a meeting with Pinard to supply the fort with opium,' stated Luke.

'So he's the rotten apple in the barrel,' said Zapote, thoughtfully. 'I must admit I thought it was somebody else.'

'What about my journey tomorrow?' demanded Luke. 'There's no way I'm going to leave here without taking Maria with me.'

'You can rest assured you won't be going to Fort Manton tomorrow,' stated Zapote, positively. 'I will have arranged a little diversion for Ricardo.'

Chapter 15

Luke was torn between his desire to see and speak to Maria and the necessity for him to keep a low profile and to pretend that he had no interest at all in her. He knew that Ricardo's spies were everywhere and that they would instantly spot and report any clandestine meeting which he arranged to have with Maria. He finally hit on the idea of having a meeting with her in the open. That way Ricardo's suspicions wouldn't be aroused.

Camilla and Penelope were in attendance as he had expected when he strolled up to Maria's tent. Although they were both in their early twenties, they appeared older, due to Mexican women maturing earlier. They greeted him deferentially, after all he was the victor in the pistol duel yesterday and as such had become the camp celebrity.

'Can I see Maria?' he enquired, politely.

'I'm afraid she's asleep,' said Camilla. 'She spends a lot of her time sleeping.'

You mean drugged, he mentally added.

'I'll come back again,' said Luke, turning away. As he did so Maria appeared in the entrance to the tent. Although Luke was steeled to accept her appearance, he was still shocked by what he saw.

Whereas normally she had a lovely round face, her cheeks were now sunken. Her eyes, which had always been bright and vivacious, were now dull and vacant. Her long fair hair which she had combed regularly, now hung limply. There was no sheen to her skin – she looked ten years older. She had lost a considerable amount of weight, and her clothes now hung on her. Luke guessed that she was hardly eating anything – the effect of the drugs was to take away a person's appetite. He swore for the umpteenth time that he would make Ricardo pay for what he was doing to her.

They stared at each other for a long time. Luke thought that he recognized some response in her gaze.

'I've brought you a book,' he ventured.

'A book?' she said, vaguely.

He produced the volume. For some strange reason he had kept it in his saddle-bag. It was *Don Quixote*, by Cervantes. It was a heavy volume and she accepted it with both hands. She stared at it with incomprehension, then gradually her expression changed. Luke could see the recognition fleeting across her face. It was almost immediately replaced by an expression of fear. She glanced at him. She gave an almost imperceptible shake of the head.

At that moment Ricardo appeared on the scene. 'Ah, the teacher still trying to instruct his pupil, I see.' Although the observation was delivered in even tones, Luke detected a warning behind the words.

'It's an occupational hazard,' stated Luke, blandly.

Ricardo took the book from Maria's hands. She flinched at his touch. 'I believe Don Quixote dies in the end,' he observed, as he idly flipped through the pages.

'Not before he realizes that he is just a man and not a controller of people's destinies.'

For a moment Luke thought he had gone too far. Ricardo's face darkened and twisted into a scowl. He stared intently at Luke, his breathing was uneven. Camilla and Penelope, sensing a confrontation, stepped back into the tent, dragging Maria with them. Luke had sensed that the ever-present lieutenants already had their hands on their guns. He, himself, was defenceless, since his guns were in his tent. Finally, after what seemed like an eternity, Ricardo nodded several times. The tension gradually evaporated. His lieutenants wiped their sweaty palms on their trousers.

'Take care, gringo, or you will go too far,' was Ricardo's parting shot as he turned on his heel and strode away.

Back in his tent Luke settled down for his afternoon siesta. It was a habit he had slipped into when he had first arrived in San Caldiz. However his rest was disturbed by wild dreams. He dreamed that he and Maria were riding together. At first their ride was very pleasant, and they were laughing and joking. Then suddenly they were riding through a valley, and everything changed. Strange wooden buildings appeared in front of them. No matter where they turned they could not avoid them. Suddenly the buildings changed into windmills. They were large and threatening and as their sails went round they threatened to knock them off their horses. Luke woke up in a cold sweat.

Any hope Luke had of going back to sleep was dashed by the arrival of Zapote. As usual he did not waste any words. 'Will you come with me tonight to show me the way to the poppy-fields?' he asked.

'What do you intend to do?' demanded Luke.

'In the words of one of the great English admirals, "I'm going to spike Ricardo's guns",' said Zapote, enigmatically.

Luke hesitated. Whatever Zapote had in mind, there was obviously an element of danger in it. However, against that was the fact that it could be a blow against Ricardo. And anything which would help to destroy Ricardo was a consummation devoutly to be wished. 'You can count on me,' he heard himself say.

Chapter 16

Zapote came for Luke at midnight. 'I've got a couple of horses in the field,' he whispered. He waited while Luke strapped on his guns.

They crept away from the silent tents towards the field where the horses were grazing. There was enough light from the faint moon to pick them out. They had their saddles on ready and in a few moments the two were riding cautiously away from the camp.

When they were out of range of the camp, Zapote asked, 'Do you think they'll have any guards on the opium stores?'

'They had guards there yesterday,' Luke informed him. 'I think we'd better assume there'll be permanent guards.'

'In that case we'll leave the horses about half

a mile from the camp and go ahead on foot,' stated Zapote.

Luke chose a suitable place to leave the horses. 'When we get beyond the ridge,' he explained, 'you'll see the poppy-fields.'

They walked for a couple of hundred yards until they breasted the ridge. They stopped and stared at the poppies which shone dully in the moonlight. Luke pointed to the low buildings to the right. 'That's where they're stored,' he informed Zapote.

They crept forward cautiously. Zapote had taken a wicked-looking knife out of a sheath. 'If there are guards, don't shoot them. It will make too much noise,' he explained.

There was no sign of the guards and for a fleeting moment Luke harboured the thought that perhaps Ricardo hadn't bothered to keep a guard on the sheds at night. In fact they had almost reached the door of the first shed when a figure rose up in front of them.

'Who are you?' he demanded. His words were given added emphasis by the rifle which he held at the ready in his hands.

Luke's mind worked at lightning speed. 'I'm Ricardo's guest,' he replied. 'I was here yesterday with Ricardo. We're partners. I've got to check something before I go to Fort Manton.'

As Luke had hoped Zapote was sidling imperceptibly forward as Luke was speaking. He was also moving to the side, thus forcing the guard to turn slightly to keep an eye on him. Luke also stepped forward.

'Keep still,' commanded the guard. 'Or I will shoot.'

It was the last command he gave. The problem of trying to watch the two of them caused him to swing the carbine back to cover Luke. Zapote timed his lightning move perfectly. He lunged forward and sank his knife into the guard's heart. He collapsed with only a faint sound.

'We'll make a good team,' said Zapote, as he wiped his knife on some grass.

'There could be another guard,' warned Luke.

Sure enough another guard came round the corner, tucking his shirt into his trousers as he did so. Even by the faint moonlight his expression of surprise was clearly to be seen. Zapote's deadly knife again found its target. 'I wonder if there are any more?' he asked aloud.

They searched the sheds, but saw no further human activity. Zapote finally focused his attention on the poppy-crusher which held pride of place in the smaller shed. 'What are you going to do?' whispered Luke.

'I'm going to make sure that this little toy will be out of action for a long time,' said Zapote. He produced a couple of large rocks and proceeded to try to put them through the machine. The handle refused to turn and the ratchets refused to grip. 'Give me a hand,' said Zapote. They both grabbed the handle and tried to turn it. The stones resisted their attempt. The two of them grunted as they applied even more pressure. 'I think it's coming,' gasped Zapote.

Sure enough, with a horrible screeching, grinding sound the ratchets sprang apart. At the same time the machine tumbled off its stand. It lay on the floor, a twisted heap of metal. 'That'll make sure that Ricardo doesn't produce any more opium on that machine,' said Zapote, with a grin. Luke, too, was grinning like a schoolboy who had been out on an illicit adventure.

'That's a good night's work,' acknowledged Luke as they stood outside the shed. The fresh air was like wine to their skin, as it cooled their sweaty brows.

'Thanks for your help,' said Zapote.

'We *do* make a good team,' said Luke, with a grin.

'There's one other thing I've got to do,' said Zapote, 'but I can do this alone.'

'You mean we haven't finished yet?' demanded Luke.

'You've finished,' Zapote corrected him. 'You've done more than enough. You go back to camp. It's important that you keep out of any further danger so that you'll be able to take your girl-friend to freedom.'

Luke wondered what further plan Zapote had in mind. However, if he wished to carry it out on his own, then who was he to argue? They had obviously achieved the main part of their objective. As the great English sailor Drake would have said, they had spiked Ricardo's guns.

Luke rode away giving Zapote a wave as he did so. They must have put Ricardo's opium production back six months. Without the crusher he would have to resort to the primitive way of cutting the capsules by hand. This would mean going back to the old slow process. It would mean that Ricardo would no longer have large quanti-ties of opium to try to snare innocent victims.

Before Luke descended into the valley which led into the camp he glanced behind him. To his surprise the sky was beginning to turn red. It took him a few seconds to realize the significance of what he was seeing. When he did he burst into laughter. Zapote had set fire to the sheds. Not only had he spiked Ricardo's guns, he had also singed the King of Spain's beard. Luke laughed until the tears ran down his face. He was still chuckling to himself when he slipped into his tent and prepared for bed.

Chapter 17

Luke was awakened by his tent flap being torn violently open. In fact the whole tent shook as if it was about to collapse. Ricardo stood in the opening. Even in the faint light of dawn Luke could see enough of his face to read his anger. Even if his face was not completely visible, his clenched fists revealed his pent-up emotion.

'You. Come with me,' he snarled.

Accompanied by his two lieutenants he led the way to the compound where the horses were kept. Luke glanced casually at the piebald horse which he had ridden to the poppy-fields. There was nothing to connect him with the horse. His own white horse was peacefully grazing in a far corner of the field.

'Get your horse,' commanded Ricardo.

In a few minutes they were riding towards the poppy-fields. There was no sign of the glow which had lit up the sky last night. In fact Luke was almost beginning to wonder whether he had dreamed the whole thing, when they breasted the ridge and he was able to see the devastation ahead.

Of the half a dozen long sheds, four had been completely burned to the ground. One was still standing intact, and the other was half burnt away. Zapote had certainly done a good job, acknowledged Luke, concealing a smile with an effort.

'We harboured a traitor who was responsible for this.' Ricardo threw out an arm with a dramatic gesture which encompassed the whole damage.

'How much did you save?' demanded Luke, with what he hoped was concern in his voice.

'Some,' snapped Ricardo.

'Enough for me to continue with our arrangements?' demanded Luke, hardly able to keep the glee out of his voice.

'Not only has he burned down the sheds, but he had also destroyed the crusher,' snarled Ricardo.

I know, thought Luke, happily. I was there.

'There is only one bright spot on the horizon,' announced Ricardo. For some reason which Luke couldn't fathom, the three of them were staring at him. Surely there was no way they could connect him with last night's happenings? He tried to look unconcerned, although his stomach churned at the menace in their combined stares. 'Come this way,' commanded Ricardo.

They rode about half a mile away from the scene. At first Luke didn't see it, then the fact that a soldier was standing nearby with a carbine alerted him to the fact that something was amiss. Ricardo dismounted a short distance from the soldier and the others automatically followed suit. Still Luke didn't notice why they were approaching the soldier. Suddenly Ricardo stopped. Then the full horror of the scene in front of them hit Luke.

He had heard of Indians treating their captives like this to get them to talk, but he had never viewed it at close quarters. He had to restrain himself from being violently sick. Zapote's head was the only part of him that could be seen sticking out of an ant hill. Luke was vaguely aware that Ricardo was talking.

'He was the snake in the grass I was talking about. Unfortunately for him he was caught before he had succeeded in burning down all the sheds. The ants will soon be starting to eat at his flesh. When they do so he will start screaming for help. Oh, not to get him out of the pit, but to put him out of his agony with a bullet.'

Luke couldn't trust himself to speak.

'I think he had an accomplice,' continued Ricardo, remorselessly. 'When he reveals the name of his accomplice I will put him out of his misery. Won't I, Zapote?' concluded Ricardo, kicking some sand in the man's face before turning on his heel.

Luke was sitting in his tent and absorbing the terrible turn of events. One thing was sure, he couldn't leave Zapote to his slow death of being eaten by the ants. He knew he would have to do something about it. The earliest he would be able to take action would be that night. He'd creep out of the camp again, the same way as he had the night before. Of course, once he had helped Zapote to escape, his own position would be revealed as somebody who was definitely against Ricardo and his drug trade.

What about Maria? If he was forced to flee from the camp, he couldn't leave her behind. She was due to marry the half-wit, Paulo, when he and the *padre* appeared. He couldn't leave her to that fate. Added to which was the indisputable fact that he was in love with her himself.

Without having any definite idea how he could resolve his problem he went over to Maria's tent. Only one of her usual two attendants, Camilla, was there. She demurred when Luke stated that he wanted to see Maria.

'I'm not supposed to let anyone see her,' she explained.

'It's not as if she's going to go far, is it?' asked Luke, reasonably. 'Not in her state.'

'Oh, all right,' Camilla concurred. 'Come inside the tent and stay there. Don't let anybody see you. Penelope is ill, and I'm going over to see if she's all right.'

So saying she disappeared, leaving Luke alone in the tent with Maria. She looked much as she had looked yesterday, haggard. Although when Camilla had disappeared her first words staggered Luke.

'Well don't just stand there,' she stated, calmly. 'Aren't you going to kiss me?'

'But ... but ... I thought ...' stammered Luke.

'You thought I was drugged up to my eyeballs, but I'm not. As you can hear I'm perfectly lucid.'

'But . . . but . . . how?' demanded Luke.

'I'll tell you after I've had that kiss,' Maria said, tartly.

Luke was overwhelmed by the fact that Maria seemed to be in her right senses. The fact was confirmed by their long, lingering kiss.

'I think I'd better tell you now,' stated Maria, 'I soon realized that they were going to try to keep me drugged – that way there was no danger of me trying to escape. Luckily, they decided to keep me drugged by using the liquid opium. Penelope and Camilla didn't like the idea of using a hypodermic, so they used to give me a spoonful of the liquid in the morning and the same in the evening. I pretended to take it, but insisted that I had to have something sweet to take the taste away. When they were busy searching for a toffee, I could usually manage to spit out the drug. As you can see the tent is quite dark and they couldn't see exactly what I was doing. Once I started pretending I was drugged, they lost interest in trying to make sure I had my daily dosage. On a couple of occasions I convinced them that I had already taken my 'medication' as they called it, whereas in fact I hadn't. As long as I acted the part of a drug-addict they were quite happy.'

'Well, you certainly fooled me,' said Luke, putting his arm around her waist.

'My aim was to fool everybody, especially Ricardo and Paulo,' stated Maria. 'I even stopped eating so that they would think the drug was having its effect. I've hardly eaten anything for nearly a week.' There was a childish whine in her voice which reminded Luke that although she seemed a very self-possessed woman who had carried out her plan to perfection, underneath she was still a young girl, with a craving for food.

'Now it's time for me to bring you up to date,' stated Luke. He told her about his and Zapote's venture, and how Zapote had been caught, and was facing an excruciatingly slow death.

'What are we going to do?' demanded Maria.

'Now that I know you are well, we've got to escape from the camp tonight. We'll collect Zapote and we'll head for San Caldiz. With luck we'll be half-way there before Ricardo realizes we're missing and starts coming after us.'

Somehow any further conversation was curtailed by another long, lingering kiss.

Chapter 18

That night Luke waited impatiently for the minutes to tick away before it would be safe for him to venture outside his tent. He had planned to wait until midnight, the time that he and Zapote had set out the previous night. At last the hour arrived and Luke cautiously opened the flap of his tent. He was taken aback by the sight that met his eyes. There were two armed guards outside his tent.

'Where are you going, *señor*?' demanded one of them.

'I'm – I couldn't sleep, so I'm going for a walk,' stammered Luke.

'Ricardo's orders are that you do not leave the tent,' said the second guard, emphasizing his statement by raising his rifle, threateningly.

Luke knew that he could take one of them, but not both. At least not before the second would have raised the alarm. Cursing under his breath Luke went back into the tent.

This had put the cat among the pigeons. All his plans to rescue Zapote and ride with him and Maria to safety had been nullified at one stroke. It was obvious that Ricardo seriously considered the possibility that he had been Zapote's accomplice. And he intended keeping him under close observation until Zapote was forced to scream out his name when the ants had eaten far enough into his flesh.

He could visualize Maria waiting for him impatiently. He could guess at her frustration. She was in the worse position of not knowing why he hadn't come for her as he had promised. She would imagine all kinds of mishaps which could have befallen him – ranging from sudden sickness to instant death. He smacked his fists in frustration as he paced up and down the tent.

Maria, in fact, had accidentally discovered the reason for his non-appearance. Penelope had arranged to stay with her friend Camilla for the night. This suited Maria's plans since she would be alone in the tent, and therefore able to slip out when Luke appeared. Camilla was what was

euphemistically called 'sick' although her real
complaint was that she was expecting a baby at
any time. So when Penelope had left the tent,
Maria had joyfully assumed that Luke's plan
was going ahead. However a hitch soon appeared
when Penelope poked her head back inside the
tent.

'There are two armed guards outside Luke's
tent,' she announced. 'I wonder what he's been
up to.'

So Luke wouldn't be coming to her tent
tonight, in order that they could make their
escape. Luke was obviously under suspicion for
his and Zapote's excursion. Ricardo was waiting
until the ants had eaten into Zapote's flesh when
he would reach the point that he would scream
out the name of his accomplice in order to see the
end of his pain. Maria knew it was only a matter
of hours. She had seen Indians torture their
enemies this way. They used to say that no man
can survive more than a few hours after the ants
had began to eat their flesh.

Dawn crept into Luke's tent. He hadn't slept.
He had stopped pacing up and down hours ago,
but his mind was still churning like a river-boat
engine.

His guns were loaded and ready. He had

decided that if it came to a fight, at least he'd take Ricardo with him, whether the guards succeeded in getting in a shot first or not. Ricardo was the most evil man he had ever come across and that included all the fictional evil characters he could bring to mind.

His breakfast was brought in to him on a tray as usual – a cup of coffee and some fresh tortillas. Normally he would have devoured the warm tortillas hungrily, since they had not long been baked by some of the women in the camp. This morning, however, he pushed them to one side impatiently.

Luke knew there was nothing he could do except wait. About the middle of the morning the two guards were changed. He heard them laughing and joking as their replacements took over. They were fortunate to have something to laugh about, thought Luke, morosely. His days for laughter were over. He was convinced that Ricardo would soon come to the tent and announce that Zapote had revealed that he, Luke, had been his accomplice. Then the whole cock-and-bull story about him being an assistant for a drug-dealer in the cavalry would be blown. Any hopes he had harboured about escaping with Maria would be shattered. All that would be left was to ensure that when the time came for him to die, that he would take Ricardo with him.

It was some time in the afternoon when Ricardo came for him. As usual he was accompanied by his two lieutenants. Luke had strapped on his guns and Ricardo glanced at them curiously as he entered the tent.

Ricardo didn't come to the point straight away. 'I hear you didn't eat your breakfast,' he said, casually.

So Ricardo wanted to play a cat-and-mouse game, did he? 'I couldn't stomach the thought of food while that poor soul was being eaten alive by ants,' snapped Luke.

'You shouldn't waste your sympathy on a traitor,' stated Ricardo, bluntly.

Luke's hand was hovering near his pistol. The two lieutenants were holding their guns casually. No doubt the last thing they expected was that Luke would shoot their beloved leader in front of their eyes. But that was what he was going to do once Ricardo revealed that Zapote had named him as his accomplice.

'The *padre* has arrived in the camp,' said Ricardo. 'Everything will soon be arranged for my son, Paulo, to marry the beautiful Maria. You find her beautiful, yes?'

'I haven't an opinion one way or the other,' Luke lied through his teeth. 'To me she was just my pupil.'

'I am disappointed in my son,' said Ricardo, reflectively. 'I had hoped he would make a soldier like me. Instead he is a weakling. Still, one never knows; if Maria has a son by him, then perhaps he will grow up to be strong and clever like his grandfather.'

Luke's fingers were now touching his gun. He knew that in a few seconds Ricardo would give up playing this cat-and-mouse game.

'You must come to the wedding,' stated Ricardo. 'We will have a grand fiesta. It will last a whole week.'

Why was Ricardo inviting him to the wedding? Did it mean that Zapote hadn't revealed his name to him?

To Luke's surprise Ricardo turned to leave the tent. Was it a trick to lure him off his guard? Ricardo's remark before he left the tent took him completely aback. 'Zapote has revealed the name of his accomplice,' stated Ricardo. 'It's Velarde.'

Chapter 19

Luke was ready at midnight once again. He hoped that Maria had heard the news about Zapote naming Velarde as the traitor. It was obvious that Zapote had considered Velarde's life as worthless compared with Luke's and so he had chosen to lie, rather than sacrifice Luke to the not too tender mercies of Ricardo.

To Luke's relief Maria was waiting for him just inside her tent. He gave her a quick kiss, then told her they would be taking three of the horses from the compound. She didn't demur as he led the way to the horses.

Ten minutes later they were riding towards the poppy-fields, with Luke leading Zapote's horse. The moon was almost full and so gave them a clear view of their objective. When they came to the burnt out sheds, Maria regarded them with surprise. 'Zapote did this?' she inquired.

'Yes, and he has suffered for his venture,' Luke stated, shortly.

Maria glanced at him, keenly. Was he feeling guilty about leaving Zapote behind to carry out his plan on his own? Luke swung his horse away from the sheds and Maria followed him.

To Luke's relief there were no guards on the ant hills. It was obvious that Ricardo had assumed that that chapter of events was now closed, and so there was no need to mount a guard. Zapote's head was easy to find. To Luke's surprise he seemed to be asleep. Luke knelt down by him. There were red ants everywhere, crawling over his face. Maria gave a gasp of horror when she realized there were hundreds of them scurrying around.

Zapote opened his eyes. Luke brushed some of the ants away which were getting in his mouth. 'I fooled them,' Zapote croaked. 'Now you have a chance to escape.'

'I'll dig you out,' said Luke, grimly. 'I've brought your horse.'

'It's too late,' whispered Zapote. 'The ants are eating away at my flesh. There's only one thing to do now.'

The Bandit Trail

'For heaven's sake, get it over,' cried Maria.

'Are you sure?' Luke asked Zapote.

'Yes, I made my peace with my Maker when I saw you coming.'

Luke drew his gun. He held it to Zapote's head. 'We put Ricardo's opium production back six months, didn't we?' were Zapote's last words before Luke put his gun to his head and pulled the trigger.

They found Velarde about a hundred yards away. He was stretched out on top of an ant hill. 'Cut me free,' he cried, 'the ants haven't started getting at me yet.'

A few moments later he was rubbing his wrists and cursing Zapote. 'He did this to me,' he whined.

'Well he's dead now,' stated Luke. 'He was a friend of mine, and if you don't stop whining, you'll be joining him,' he added, pointing his gun at Velarde.

'Hey! I'm a friend of yours, too,' protested Velarde.

'All right, let's not quarrel,' said Maria, placatingly. 'We've got to get out of here.'

Velarde noticed the spare horse. 'Take me with you,' he pleaded. 'If I stay here, Ricardo will surely kill me.'

Luke considered the request.

'I know the paths up on the hills,' added Velarde. 'I know them like the back of my hand. That way you'll be able to reach San Caldiz safely.'

'He's got a point there,' Luke informed Maria. 'We'll have to take to the hills when Ricardo sends his men after us.'

'All right, only let's get out of here,' said Maria, impatiently.

They rode like the wind to put as much distance between themselves and the bandits' camp before dawn, when Ricardo would discover that they were missing. They were following the wide trail that Luke and Velarde had followed when they had travelled to the bandits' camp a few days before. Luke knew that Velarde was right and that some time during the day they would have to strike up into the hills to avoid their pursuers. Because as sure as God made little green apples Ricardo and his bandits would follow them. They would have two scores to settle, one to get even with him for helping Zapote to avoid the slow, painful death that Ricardo had planned for him. And also to recover the runaway bride to be, Maria. A third possibility was that Ricardo had guessed by now that it was he, and not Velarde, who had ruined his poppy-crushing machine.

'When are we going to take to the hills?' Maria asked the question about mid-morning, when the heat was beginning to hold them in its scorching grip.

'Which is the best path to follow?' Luke asked Velarde.

'About a couple of miles further on, there's a narrow path which leads up into the hills. If you don't know it's there, you'll miss it,' he explained.

Sure enough neither Luke nor Maria noticed the path as Velarde suddenly swung to the right. Soon they were climbing steadily. At least they knew that when they reached the top of the mountain the air would be cooler.

The bandits came for them in the late afternoon. They could see the riders clearly from their vantage point a couple of thousand feet above the plain. Luke counted thirteen. He wondered whether it was an unlucky omen.

The bandits couldn't see them and had soon passed them by. 'We'll ride for another hour or so,' said Luke. 'Then we'll rest the horses for the day. They've had a tiring journey and we'll want them fresh again in the morning.'

'I agree,' said Velarde. 'The bandits will ride

on for some time until they realize that we are not ahead of them. By the time they turn back it'll be too late for them to attack us this evening.'

'When do you think they will attack?' asked Maria, fearfully.

'In the morning,' replied Velarde. 'But do not fear for your safety. I am a good shot.'

They lit a fire and Maria cooked some beans. Luke noticed that she wolfed them down as if she hadn't eaten for days. Then he remembered how she had explained that she had refrained from eating food in order to maintain the impression that she was taking drugs.

When they settled down for the night Velarde rolled up in his blanket a discreet distance away from them. Luke arranged his blanket a couple of feet away from Maria's.

'Why are you lying over there?' she whispered.

'I thought — perhaps — you'd rather not be disturbed,' he whispered in return.

'I'm cold,' she said. She moved over until she was close against him. It seemed inevitable that they should start to kiss. Then later it was just as inevitable that they should explore each other's bodies.

Later, when they were resting and staring at

the stars he said, 'You seem to have learned a lot in the convent school.'

'I learned a lot from the books you loaned me,' she replied.

'Are you sure those things were in the books?' he enquired, innocently.

'I read between the lines,' she said, as she leaned over to give him a goodnight kiss.

The bandits started climbing up towards them at first light.

'They're not wasting any time,' observed Velarde, as he took aim with the rifle Luke had given him, which he had taken from the guards a couple of nights before.

'Wait until I give the order to shoot,' said Luke. 'We don't want to waste any bullets.'

Luke watched them slowly climbing up the mountainside. It was easy to pick Ricardo out since he was wearing a colourful shirt. However he was also keeping to the rear of the climbers, urging them forwards.

It was obvious that Velarde was getting itchy to start shooting.

'You have to get at least two of them with your first shots to cut down the odds,' whispered Luke. 'I'll take the two on the left. You take the two on the right. When I give the word, you shoot.'

The bandits were within range of their rifles but Luke knew that he and Velarde would have to wait for them to climb higher up the mountain before they could be sure of killing at least two of them. Maria had moved over to where Velarde was lying and she began to whisper something to him. It was obvious to Luke that she was distracting him and trying to get him to hold his fire until the bandits were nearer.

Finally Luke judged that the moment had arrived. He took careful aim at the bandit on the far left.

'Fire,' Luke commanded. Their rifle shots sounded as one. Luke was relieved to see that he had hit the bandit he had aimed at. He followed it up with a quick snap shot at the second. This shot was just as accurate and the bandit tumbled back down the mountain after giving an unearthly scream.

Luke glanced across to see how Velarde had fared. The bandit he had been aiming at was lying unnaturally still on the mountainside. 'Three down, ten to go,' whispered Luke.

'I got him, didn't I?' exclaimed Velarde, excitedly.

'Yes, but keep your head down, or he'll be the last one you'll get,' advised Luke, drily.

After the initial shooting the bandits had gone to ground. 'What do you think they'll do now?' demanded Maria.

'They'll try and creep up until they can get behind us,' said Luke. 'It'll take them some time. Whenever one of them makes a mistake and puts his head up too high, blow it off,' he ordered Velarde.

Velarde gave him a wide grin. He was obviously enjoying himself. It's nice to see that one of us is doing so, thought Luke as he reviewed the seriousness of the situation.

They might be able to pick off another couple of the bandits. But that would still leave eight. More than enough to eventually outflank them and then their chances of survival would be pretty thin.

Because of the treacherous nature of the terrain the bandits had left their horses below on the plain, while they climbed up to try to get to terms with Luke and Velarde. Luke came to a sudden decision.

'We've got to get out of here, before they trap us,' he told Velarde. 'We'll ride along the ridge. They'll have to go back down to get their horses.

It'll give us a couple of hours' lead.'

Luke put his plan into action. They were soon galloping along the ridge, leaving the frustrated bandits to fire a few wayward shots after them. When they were safely out of immediate danger, Luke asked: 'Is there a good place along the trail where we'll be able to ambush them?'

'There's a good place about six miles ahead,' replied Velarde. 'The trail narrows, and we can take up our positions and wait for them.'

'It sounds perfect,' said Luke.

It was.

'Let's hope Ricardo still thinks we're up on the mountain,' said Luke, as they took up their positions and began to wait.

It was about an hour later when the bandits appeared down the trail.

'Wait until I give the order to shoot,' whispered Luke.

Again he was disappointed to see that Ricardo was bringing up the rear. However, he sighted his rifle on one of the front riders.

'Fire!' he yelled.

This time they hit two of the bandits. The remainder didn't hesitate – they turned tail and fled.

'They're running away,' said Velarde, excitedly.

He was so carried away by their success that he raised his head above the level of his hiding-place. It was a fatal mistake. It gave Ricardo an easy target. He took it. Velarde collapsed in a pool of his own blood.

'Let's get away from here,' said a distressed Maria.

CHAPTER 20

Chapter 20

A couple of days later Luke was sitting in Marshal Downley's office. Captain Manuel Torsa was also present.

'You say you've been to Ricardo's camp, and you've lived to tell the tale,' stated an astonished Downley.

'Yes, thanks to a clever, brave man named Zapote,' said Luke, bitterly.

'He was a government agent,' Torsa explained. 'He was leader of the team the governor set up to fight the growing drug menace.'

'He was brave enough to burn down Ricardo's sheds after we had damaged his opium-crusher,' stated Luke.

'You helped him?' enquired Downley.

'My contribution was negligible,' said Luke, shortly.

Torsa produced a map. 'Could you mark where the opium-fields lie?' he asked.

It was a poorly drawn map, but Luke could distinguish where the fields would lie in relation to the surrounding hills. He pointed them out. 'There,' he said.

Torsa examined the spot with interest. 'If I could get a platoon of soldiers, do you think we could destroy the camp?'

'I'm sure you could,' said Luke. 'Ricardo's bandits are no fighters. That showed when they ran off after we had ambushed them.'

'How long would it take the soldiers to get there?' asked Downley.

'Two days' hard riding,' said Luke.

Torsa's next question took Luke by surprise. 'Would you ride with us, to make sure that we do not lose our way? You will of course be paid for the expedition.'

Maria was dead against him going. 'It's nothing to do with you,' she protested, when he had returned to the villa. 'It's none of your business. It's all over now.'

'Ricardo is still alive,' he reminded her. 'It's unfinished business.'

'But what if you get hurt? Or, worse, what if you get killed?' she wailed.

150

'I've got to see that Ricardo is killed. For what he did to Zapote.'

'But it's soldiers' work,' she protested tearfully. 'You're a civilian. It's none of your business.'

'I've got to go,' he said, stubbornly.

'I've only just found you, and now you're leaving me.' She tried to hold the tears back.

'I won't be away long. Four days maybe. Just long enough to see that Ricardo gets his just desserts.' She rushed from the room.

Luke had arranged to meet Torsa and his soldiers in the square. He checked his guns. There was no sign of Maria after he had strapped them on and was about to lead his horse to join Torsa and his men. Luke cast a last longing glance at Maria's bedroom before leading his horse out through the gates. There was no sign of her.

Torsa had arranged for the platoon of soldiers to leave in style. He had mustered a small band from somewhere. There were a handful of pipe-players and a drummer. They weren't the best band that Luke had heard by a long way, but what they lacked in technique they made up in enthusiasm.

The band were fittingly playing 'The Girl I Left Behind Me', as Torsa put the finishing

touches to his platoon. Luke had counted
twenty-two soldiers. He knew that Ricardo could
put three times that number against them. But
whether or not they would have the stomach to
fight was another question.

Torsa gave the order, 'Platoon, ready.'

Luke gave one last despairing glance in the
direction of the villa. He had hoped she would be
here to see him off. It was obvious, though, that
she didn't understand what was driving him to
see Ricardo killed. He knew it was a primitive
desire for revenge, that he would not rest until it
had been satisfied.

Suddenly a figure in white was hurtling across
the square. Torsa was on the point of giving the
command to ride when he paused. Luke jumped
down from his horse to greet Maria. She leaped
into his arms to a round of applause from the
soldiers. Even Torsa permitted himself a smile.

'Come back safely, darling,' said Maria, after
their kiss was over.

'I promise,' said Luke, with a wave of his hand
as they moved off.

Ricardo was waiting for them, as Luke had half-
guessed he would be. He had arranged his
bandits in a circle around the camp, which made

it more difficult for Torsa and his men to attack. Torsa consulted Luke as to their best move.

'If we attack from the front,' said Torsa, 'he will surely kill half a dozen of my men before we can get near him.'

'He's made one mistake already,' stated Luke, as he thoughtfully studied the bandits arraigned against them.

'What's that?' demanded a puzzled Torsa.

'He's spread out his men so that they're too far apart.'

'But I will lose too many men by the time we arrive at their lines,' said a disappointed Torsa. He had expected the ex-cavalry soldier to come up with an idea, but so far Luke had not responded.

'Oh, we don't attack them,' stated Luke. 'We make them attack us.'

'And how do you propose to make them do that?' demanded Torsa, who had began privately to hold the view that it had been a waste of time in bringing the tall American with them. Except, of course that he had shown them where the bandit camp was.

'There are still two sheds standing where Ricardo is storing his poppies,' said Luke. 'We will burn them down. Ricardo will come out to attack us to try to prevent the loss of the rest of his precious flowers. And we will hold the upper hand. Not only that, the sun is getting low in the sky. Your soldiers will have their backs to the sun, but it will be in the eyes of the bandits. It will give your men another advantage.'

Torsa had to admit that it was not a bad idea. 'Where are the poppy-fields?' he demanded.

'I will show you,' stated Luke.

They made a detour round the camp and finally arrived at the poppy-fields. There were only half a dozen bandits guarding the sheds and after a quick skirmish three were lying dead and the other three were running away. Luke prevented one of the soldiers from firing at the fleeing bandits. 'We want them to tell Ricardo what has happened,' he pointed out. 'Soon I think the bandits will return. This time we will be waiting for them.'

While they were waiting Torsa ordered his men to destroy the poppies in the fields with their swords.

'You said that Zapote said that he had put Ricardo's plans back six months,' stated Torsa. 'This will put them back for ever.' He vigorously sliced through several plants at one stroke.

Ricardo and his bandits came at them like

madmen. They had seen their livelihood disappearing up in smoke and now the soldiers were destroying the last remains of their comfortable life. The bandits knew that with the loss of their poppy-fields they would have to go back to scraping a pitiful existence from the barren soil.

Torsa had arranged his men in two rows, as he had read in his text-books that that was the way the most successful modern army, the British army, would align their soldiers. The first row was kneeling and the second row stood behind them. At Torsa's command the two rows fired. The result was a withering concentration of fire-power, which stopped the bandits in their tracks. It took them only a few seconds to realize that the cause for which they had been enthusiastically fighting a few minutes ago wasn't worth dying for. They turned tail and retreated. Luke was pleased to see that Torsa did not command his men to cut them down as they fled. There were enough dead bandits lying on the battlefield already.

Luke had spotted Ricardo riding off on his black horse. He grabbed one of the soldiers' horses and galloped off after him. Ricardo's horse, as befitted the horse of a leader, was a superb racing stallion. Luke knew that he didn't stand a chance of catching him as the distance between them inexorably widened.

Luke had resigned himself to losing his quarry when suddenly, inexplicably, Ricardo's horse stumbled. Ricardo shot over its head. Luke rode towards the scene, drawing his pistol as he did so.

A shot a couple of inches past Luke's head reminded him that even a wounded Ricardo was a dangerous one. Luke rolled off his horse in a movement that he had practised hundreds of times when in the cavalry. His old instructor would have been proud of him, he thought, as he continued rolling so as not to present a stationary target.

Ricardo's bullets peppered the ground around him, but failed to find their target. Luke sought safety in a hollow where he was temporarily able to assess the situation.

Ricardo's horse was some distance away and from the way it was moving, it had obviously damaged a tendon. So Ricardo wouldn't be able to make a quick escape, Luke was pleased to note. All he had to do was to keep Ricardo pinned down until Torsa and his soldiers arrived. They would capture Ricardo. And that would be the end of the villain, at least until the hangman let him drop from the rope.

Luke put his plan of keeping Ricardo pinned down into action. Every few moments he would aim a shot a few inches above Ricardo's head.

Ricardo had obviously come to the same conclusion as Luke – that his moments of freedom were shortening rapidly and would come to an abrupt end when the soldiers arrived. Suddenly he sprang up and dashed, not for his own horse, but Luke's. Although Luke was taken by surprise, he soon had him in his sights. For a reason which Luke could never satisfactorily explain to himself he waited for a few seconds. Ricardo reached Luke's horse. He jumped on it. He turned round, almost in a gesture of triumph, probably assuming that Luke had run out of bullets. It was at that moment that Luke chose to shoot him between the eyes.

Torsa rode up soon after. He glanced at Ricardo. 'It's all over then,' he said.

'Yes, it's all over,' agreed Luke.

'What happened to Ricardo's horse?' demanded Torsa.

'It's a beautiful irony,' said Luke. 'The horse stumbled. It was frightened by Zapote's head. It's in the sand where Ricardo buried him.'

When they were riding slowly back to rejoin

the others Torsa said, 'You did well. You should think about taking up the business of soldiering again.'

'No thanks,' said Luke, with a smile. 'I've got some unfinished business of my own to attend to.'